Bloody Marvellous

Bloody
Marvellous

JULIAN RATHBONE

ST. MARTIN'S PRESS
NEW YORK

AUTHOR'S NOTE

Some years ago I wrote a thriller, *Diamonds Bid*, set in Turkey. Because I had lived in Turkey a few acquaintances of mine assumed that the book, fanciful though it was, was grounded in fact. It was entirely fiction. *Bloody Marvellous* is set in Sussex and Spain. During the time I spent writing it I lived in Sussex and Spain. It has no factual basis whatsoever, either in character or plot. I have even altered the date of the Feast of St Teresa of Ávila. Even the bridge players Clive and Wilf are fictional, for only in fiction do experienced bridge players bid like that.

J.R.

Part One

CHAPTER I

Saul lived in Brighton and commuted each day up to Ventleigh where we both worked in the same school; I had to pass the station on my way home, and so it was not unnatural for me to give him a lift if we happened to be leaving the school at the same time. That was the trouble with the whole unnatural adventure—its beginnings were so natural; though there were older members of the staff who felt I was too familiar with the younger teachers in my department. Perhaps they were right. Anyway, as we turned out of the car-park Saul asked me how the term had been. It was almost the end of the Spring term.

It had been murder as he well knew, but it was kind of him to give me the chance to blow off about it. I ran through it all: the mock examinations, the struggle with money at the end of the financial year, my continuing feud with the headmaster, the marking, the musical production —I had played Fagin in *Oliver*—literally a sixty hour week, and my wife had left me just before the beginning of the term. I suppose I enjoyed my little grumble, though I was near to tears at times: not with self-pity, but with sheer bloody exhaustion and the knowledge that someone was listening to me with sympathy.

'You ought to go to a party tomorrow,' he said.

'I went to one last week. After *Oliver*.'

'Crap.'

'It was a good party.' Steady now, traffic lights.

'Teachers and sixth formers? It can't have been that good.'

'Oh, I don't know. Del Quay was there.' Even then I felt a little goose-pimply at the thought of Del Quay.

'Marvellous,' said Saul. 'That girl is marvellous. The greatest thing from the States since sliced bread. We all fancy her.'

I looked at Saul—thin, gold-rimmed specs tinted violet against migraine, coarse fair hair almost to his shoulders, and a bumpy, pointed nose that occasionally glowed with dyspepsia or drink. He could, being twelve years younger than me, fancy sixth form girls or girls in their first university term without impropriety. Besides, he wasn't married, and I was—for the time being, anyway.

But he was still speaking.

'I think you should get away from it all, away from Ventleigh. I'm going to this party in Putney tomorrow night and it'll be a change for you. There'll be theatre and telly people there, you'll find it interesting. And it might even be exciting. A change anyway,' he repeated.

'I don't know.'

'Think it over. I'll be on the seven o'clock from Brighton. You can get on here. We could have a meal first.'

I pulled into the kerb outside the station.

'I'll think about it,' I said. 'But I doubt if I'll come. See you on Monday.'

He patted me on the shoulder. 'See you tomorrow,' he said, and slammed the door.

Why did I go? Boredom, frustration, loneliness? Or the feeling of emptiness, the listlessness at the end of a long and exhausting term? Perhaps, but not as a means of forgetting the heartbreak of my wife's departure three months before. There had been no heartbreak.

I had been quite content when Helen left me after six-teen years of nothing very much, even excited. We married while still up at Oxford, an unusual thing to do in those days and there had been quite a glow over us for a year or two. She got a first and wanted to do a Ph.D. at London; I failed to get into the B.B.C. and drifted, almost without thinking, into teaching. I taught in Camden Town, and Islington, and because I was an anomaly in those derelict schools in derelict areas—an Oxford graduate where there were few graduates of any sort—I was promoted. I liked the work too, particularly in those early years when I was teaching English rather than cramming kids for examina-tions. Eventually I applied for and was appointed to the Head of the Department of English at one of the three giant comprehensives in Ventleigh new town. It had to be Ventleigh, or somewhere equally close to London, because Doctor Helen Elmer, Reader in Medieval History, author of *The Technology of the Tudor Industrial Revolution* needed to live within half an hour's train journey of the Smoke.

We drifted, as they say, apart. Eighteen months after the move to Ventleigh she began to share a flat in London with the secretary to the Keeper of the Tudor Collection at the British Museum, and only came home at weekends. Then, last September, she got a senior post in her college, and found she could afford a flat of her own. By January the trip back to Ventleigh each weekend had become pointless and so she stopped making it.

No doubt she had affairs. That sort of thing is easier in University circles. I don't deny I tried too, but my circum-stances were more constrained than hers—schools like to think the lives of their teachers are above reproach. Per-haps it would have been different if we had had children, but open-cast mining in the reign of the first Elizabeth proved too engrossing for Helen and we never did.

After her departure in January I told myself I was a real bachelor, for the first time in my life. I smoked in bed, released wind freely and noisily, and bought girlie magazines. I bought fillet steak and went through the cordon bleu syllabus. And it wasn't long before I found spaghetti bolognese with half a bottle of whisky gave more satisfaction than tournedos rossini with a pricey claret. I began to drink far too much, but never until I had finished work for the day, which, as I have said, could often be as late as eleven o'clock. This meant I was pretty useless at school until midday.

Sometime in February, probably the day before half-term, I told a sixth former off for being tipsy after lunch-time and I got a rude answer.

'You have never seen me the worse for drink,' I said.

'Does that count hangovers?' was what I got back.

One new-found pleasure remained lasting. A year or so ago I discovered a silted-up harbour near Selsey, a bird sanctuary, but because Helen came back at weekends I rarely got to it. Now I could go every Saturday with glasses and the *Hamlyn Guide to Birds of Britain and Europe* and crawl about in the rain and mud watching the shelduck, the curlews, the redshanks, the godwits, the smaller sand-pipers and the plovers.

Well, the next day, Saturday, was lovely—the first week-end in April, and I motored to the bird sanctuary in quite a light frame of mind relishing the first haze of green on the hedges, the forsythia and daffodils in the tidy gardens. But when I drove down the lane past the caravan site and the church to my usual parking place in front of the vicarage I found eight cars already lined up where I expect one or two at most and, as I locked my Mini, I could hear, as well as a lark, some oaf's transistor radio.

Down on the path which follows the side of the mudflats things were worse. I could see at least twenty people and about six dogs. I headed for the spot I usually watch from first—a tiny spit of longish grass and low bushes. The grass is comfortable, one can remain almost completely concealed and the sanderlings come within fifty yards. The Saturday before I had watched a pair of reed buntings— elegant little chaps with black heads and white collars and I thought that they might nest nearby. And on my bank of long grass two humans were making the two-backed beast. I walked away disgusted.

No, I must be honest: I was depressed and filled with a sort of animal envy, rather than disgust. The girl, from what I could see of her, was pretty, and I had no doubt at all that if I had been with her I should not have given the reed buntings a second thought.

I drove back to Ventleigh and, at twenty-past seven, I was on the station waiting for the London train.

Saul said he was surprised to see me although he had had his head out of the carriage window just in case. His surprise offended me slightly: I felt it would not have been there had I been ten years younger, and this party, this adventure with strange people in a strange place was not going to do me any good at all if everyone there was going to think of me as 'dad'.

We had a couple of gins and tonics on the train and then went to a pub I remembered from my years in London. The landlord recognised me, which was gratifying, and we had a good pub meal—cold cuts off the joint, and all that. After a few more drinks we bought a bottle of vodka for the party and moved on.

Our hosts, complete strangers to me of course, lived in

13

one of those very solid, quite large, Edwardian villas between the Lower Richmond Road and the river. There were a lot of people there, perhaps a hundred or more, and they were a very mixed bunch. There were bearded weirdies, would-be weirdies with beads and bands round their foreheads, and nattily suited, after-shaved execs; there were girls in smocks and jeans, and ladies—I suppose they would like to be called ladies—in long dresses and hairdos. There were one or two pale earnest youths with dumpy, not too clean consorts, but most of them had made it, and just how well they had made it was their main topic of conversation. Our host was a producer at Thames and had known Saul years ago at the Theatre Royal, Stratford, before he had gone on to Cambridge and better things.

As far as my anxiety about my age went—well, it depends how you look at it. There was one woman, perhaps older than me, perhaps divorced or something, who was very much in the hunt.

'Can I have a light?' was her opening move.

I was sitting on the arm of a chair with a vodka and Coke taking in the ambience and there she was, stooping towards me, earrings and everything else dangling in front of my nose, a Gauloise thrust out threatening my eye. Naturally I lit her cigarette, and naturally she perched on the arm of the next chair.

'You look lonely,' she said.

'Alone but not lonely,' I smiled.

We chatted along a bit. Yes, she too was separated from her spouse; she was a freelance journalist, and so on. She was, I suppose, quite attractive, but I couldn't help noticing the tiny creases at the top of her cleavage, and the rapaciously long nails. Her name was Joselinda, or something of the sort, but she answered to Jo. After a time she suggested that we dance, and we pushed our way to a front room where a powerful stereo was belting out a Chuck Berry album.

I dance rather well—flamboyantly perhaps, a touch narcissistically, but I enjoy myself and my partners generally seem to as well. However, Jo attempted to match my prancings at the regulation distance of one metre for only one track; then, firmly, she drew herself up to me.

'I do like dancing with you,' she murmured and wriggled her stomach more tightly against me.

'Mmmmm,' I said. One tries to be polite.

She nibbled my ear, and her hand slipped towards my rump. It really wasn't the sort of music for this sort of activity.

'My house is only three doors away.'

Her perfume was loud, her mouth too moist, her body —well, I sensed the hard muscles of the keep-fit addict.

'Let me get you a drink,' I said as the album crashed to its conclusion.

Nevertheless, my ego had been rewarded—not only by the fact that a woman had found me attractive, but also because I had resisted an easy lay after some months of abstinence and on aesthetic grounds at that. I took a long drink, sampled some quite palatable cold buffet, and decided to look for metal more attractive.

Something rather interesting was going on in one of the rooms on the first floor. Normally it was a playroom or a nursery: there were low wicker chairs, low tables, a lot of cushions, a Wendy house, and there was a teddy bear propped on the mantelpiece. But it was no nursery now. Beneath one unshaded red bulb seven or eight people lay or sat about the floor in a sort of informal circle. Mostly they were the bearded and beaded brigade, but there were one or two floral shirts with large knotted ties as well.

They talked in a low murmur, hardly audible above the quiet monotony of Oriental music, and they passed between them two fat ragged cigarettes which glowed electric green beneath the red light. There was a heavy odour—foetid and sour beneath the incense of joss-sticks.

My reactions were mostly pleasant. I felt this was it, I was living it up at last. I felt pleased that the group was so quiet, so content. I felt a touch amused at the self-consciousness of it all—the red light, the Indian music. And I wondered—what if we're raided?

'They're behaving better than most of the drunks downstairs, wouldn't you say?' The speaker was about thirty, perhaps a shade more. He had a thick fashionable mop of well-groomed, glossy black hair, a striped shirt, a waistcoat, and a rather heavy gold ring. His face was tanned, richly tanned seems the right expression.

'Yes, I would.' I felt flattered, as if my views on a national problem were being canvassed by a television interviewer. I looked more closely at him—had I seen him on the box?

'You don't have strong views about the drug problem then? Forgive me, but I gathered from someone that you are a school teacher, and I would have thought...'

He spoke slowly, earnestly, in a rather deep voice, just a little like Clement Freud's, and showed a marked gap between his front teeth. I realised that I was a little drunk and that an effort would be needed to keep the conversation on the tone of moral earnestness that had been set. After all, he would, no doubt, base his opinion of state school teachers on what I said, and the reputation of my profession was at stake.

'Well, of course,' I said, 'I don't like to see children of school age taking drugs of any sort, including tobacco or drink,' absently my hand reached for my cigarettes, 'but

I imagine none of these are as young as that...'

His lighter, gold and slim, flared in front of my face.

'I wouldn't be too sure of the age of one or two here.'

I looked more closely. Certainly one or two of the girls ... but it's so difficult to tell nowadays.

'Even so,' I went on judiciously, 'this stuff is relatively harmless and nonaddictive, I gather. I should be more worried if they were on amphemat ... aphmetan ... pills. Or whisky.'

A very attractive girl, blonde, tanned, in a gold dress with gold jewellery—she looked like something out of a Martini commercial—drifted between us.

'Hallo, Mike,' she said, and snuggled into him, taking his arm. 'You're being very serious.'

'Well, yes, we are dear. My friend here—I'm sorry, I don't know your name...'

'Elmer. Mark Elmer.'

'Nice to know you, Mark. This is Caroline. Mark is a school teacher, and was just saying, very sensibly I thought, that cannabis was less dangerous to young people than amphetamines or even alcohol.'

'Of course he's right,' Caroline laughed, a sound like gold charms. 'You're an absolute pig after half a bottle of spirits, but docile as a lamb if you get high on that stuff.' She snuggled closer. 'Can't we sit down somewhere?'

She moved into the room and found a cushion against the wall away from the circle of pot-smokers. I hesitated.

'After you, old chap,' said Mike.

I sat beside her, back restfully settled against a wall decorated with a bull-fight poster, and Mike sat next to me so that I was between them. I sipped my vodka though I felt very light-headed already: perhaps I was breathing in some of the fumes.

'Of course,' said Mike, 'it's getting wickedly expensive

17

nowadays. The Customs have caught on to all the old tricks, airport security is tighter, people who travel frequently can expect to be thoroughly searched every now and then, and anyone who looks at all unconventional gets done as a matter of course.'

'It seems a shame, no, a nashnol disgrace,' I said, more to keep the conversation going than anything else—I liked these people and I felt I would be maudlinly lonely if they went. 'Young people will take to drink if it's cheaper. Far worse for them.'

'Mind you,' said Caroline, 'it's easy enough if you go on a package tour at the height of the season. With literally hundreds coming through the customs every hour, you can get away with murder if you look right.' She leant across me. 'Remember what we got back from Tangiers last August, Mike? A year's supply as moderate users.'

'Yes. And a cool thou on the market on top of that. Paid for the holiday. Mind you it's easier if you have a family.'

'Do you have a family, Mark?' asked Caroline.

'No, er no. That is, no children.'

'You should get some.'

Shortly after that they drifted away.

CHAPTER II

What happened next is not strictly relevant to the rest of my story: yet the psychological effect it had on me was, I think, decisive. The possibility of a whole new approach to life was opened up.

First of all I must enter a word of explanation. From what one reads in novels, sees on television, hears third-hand from one's younger colleagues, what happened next would seem to be scarcely worth recording, and indeed, in the light of what was to happen to me later, I'm still not sure that it is. I repeat, I insist: it had its effect on me. You see, at that time, at the age of thirty-eight, I had slept with only two women: a scruffy affair with the under-matron at a prep school I taught in before going up to Oxford, and Helen, my wife.

I lingered in the nursery for perhaps five minutes after Caroline and Mike had left before making my way down, treading carefully over the groups on the stairs who seemed to be arguing about the Argentinian writer then visiting London, to the drinks table that had been set up in the hall. Fortunately there was some vodka still left in the bottle which I had hidden in the umbrella stand.

An argument, almost a fight was developing in the small glazed vestibule inside the front door.

'It's none of your business whether my entry was a beat late or not.' This was from an attractive brunette, small, dark-eyed, wearing a rather conventional black dress. She was furious.

'It bloody well will be if you get the sack.' Her companion was a tubby young man with a moustache, wearing, of all things, a dinner jacket. 'My trombone will pay the rent, but it won't feed us.'

'Until you learn to play a decent piano your trombone won't be fit for anything but a busker's band. Are we going to this party or not?'

'Honestly Jill, I don't fancy going anywhere with you in this mood.'

'Jake. All right. You blow a lovely piano, but it was the second violins who were late...'

'But it wasn't. The late entry was on the "D" and the second...'

'Oh give me the bottle and bugger off. Jake, give me the bottle ... Oh sod it, he's gone.'

I lifted the vodka bottle out of the umbrella stand.

'Will this do?' I asked.

After all the plummy, pretentious pseuds Jill was marvellous. I poured her a stiff vodka Coke, found her some ice and, at her request, sat down on the stairs with her while she drank. She said she needed ten minutes or so to collect herself before she could enjoy the party—she did not seem at all put out that her escort had vanished.

She chattered on explosively about herself. She was the leader of the third violins in a theatre orchestra; Jake was second trombonist; she lived with him and three other musicians in a flat up Kilburn way; they had had a hard week opening at the Festival Theatre with *Carmen* and rehearsing *Tosca* and *Peter Grimes* for the repertoire; it was exciting playing opera, but now, she said, she was utterly shagged and could she have something to eat.

The buffet looked tired, but I now felt very lit up, and with Jill giggling behind me I found the kitchen. We went through the larder and chose a tin of cannelloni with parmesan cheese. While I was heating this up the hostess came in, looked at us, said, 'Oh, blast!' and went out again. A couple of beardies who had been discussing formalism in John Cage's latest work followed her. Jill giggled all the more, slipped her arms round my waist from behind, and squeezed herself against my back.

'I've talked about myself all the time,' she said later between mouthfuls. 'Who are you?'

I told her.

'I like you. And I know nobody here, so you're mine for the evening.'

Later we danced—I took my jacket off and left it somewhere—talked, smoked, and drank. Saul went by once or twice and the second time exploded with a wild snigger he uses when he finds someone's behaviour incongruous—an irritating habit. Later he got a bit wild and a couple of men pushed him out into the back garden and turned the key on him. I left him there. Meanwhile I enjoyed myself except for one desperate period of about twenty minutes. Jill went to the lavatory and then did not reappear. I went everywhere looking for her—first irritated, then angry, then filled with a desperate longing. At last I was reduced to braving ridicule and asking people if they had seen her.

'Have you seen a small girl, dark hair, quite young, wearing a black dress?'

A white-faced red head with hair frizzed out afro-style nodded past my shoulder.

'Is that her?'

And there she was.

'I've been following you for ages,' she said. 'You did

look angry. Are you like that with naughty children at school?'

There was one other incident at the party worth recording. There was a sudden commotion in the hall—'Get a doctor', 'She just needs air', 'She only lives round the corner', came from a bustling group of men, and a girl somewhere started crying. I peered over shoulders and saw Jo, the freelance journalist of a certain age, being carried out into the street feet first. She looked rather ill.

'What's wrong with her?' I asked.

'Mixing pot and strong drink,' a knowing voice replied. 'Bad habit, very.'

I felt a twinge of guilt, easily suppressed.

Not much later Jill said, 'The last train for Ventleigh must have gone ages ago.'

I supposed it had.

'You'd better come back to my place. Have you got the taxi fare?'

I had, and I hunted out my jacket from where I had dropped it.

The flat in Kilburn was large, shoddily furnished, and very untidy. Jill weaved through a living room that was littered with papers, books, clothes, unwashed crockery. She hardly glanced at Jake, the trombonist, who was snoring on a sofa under a blanket, but led me straight into a bedroom.

Many things that happened in the months that followed were to strike me as absurd, but none perhaps so much as the fact that I am eighteen years older than Jill. For the six hours and thirty-three minutes I shared her bed I felt young again, and she did nothing to bruise the illusion.

I woke about nine, pulled on some clothes, kissed her bare

shoulder, and stumbled into the living room. Jake, in a dressing-gown, was sitting at a table eating toast and reading the *Observer*. He looked up at me, eyes very serious in his round rather podgy face. Oh dear, I thought.

'Coffee?' he asked.

I agreed.

He went into a kitchen and came back with a chipped but large mug of Nescafé.

'No milk, I'm afraid. But you don't look as if you need it.'

I drank gratefully.

'Have a good time?'

'Er, yes. Thanks.'

'Jill all right?'

'Yes. She, er, enjoyed herself.'

'Good. Well, I expect you'll be off now.'

'Yes, I suppose I'd better.'

'Good. Right then.'

He led me to the door and held it open for me.

'Last night,' he said. 'My own fault really. But I don't think you'll be in touch again, will you? If you see what I mean.'

'No, I suppose not.' I felt cold at heart, but I went.

The Underground echoed hollowly to my footsteps and there was no one at the ticket office. A notice asked me to pay on arrival at my destination. The dusty electric smell of the place made me want to sneeze, and folded in my handkerchief in the top pocket of my jacket I found a printed card. 'Mike and Caroline Chichester, Commercial Agency' and an address and phone number in Twickenham. Feeling faintly puzzled I slipped the card back in the same pocket.

The lingerie advertisements looked tawdry and I thought about Jill. A warm feeling came over me and the sense of loss receded.

CHAPTER III

Term ended on the Wednesday and so there were only three teaching days left. But a lot happened in those three days—not especially exciting or significant things, not the sort of climactic events that change people's lives in novels, or even make interesting reading, but just a succession of incidents that added up to what I needed to push me over. I am going to recount them because I want it to be understood, I need to explain, just how I got into all the mess ahead of me.

It started on the Sunday. I got back to my flat at about eleven o'clock, made myself an omelette, drank some beer and went to bed, setting the alarm for four o'clock in the afternoon as I had work to do for Monday. When I awoke I felt refreshed, and much of the excitement of the previous night still lingered. Even after a shower I felt I could detect traces of Jill's perfume hanging like an aura of bliss around me, but as soon as I got out my work—a set of sixth-form essays on *Coriolanus*—a leaden weight seemed to fix itself across my back and in my arms, and my eyelids ached with the effort to keep them up. I battled on for an hour or so and then moved on to a batch of exercise books—'O' level this time and a poor group.

'Being as it was raining ... there are many aspects in modelmakeing (sic) ... like is often said, it's an ill-wind ...

the medows (sic) were lovley (sic) all covered in butter-cups like little golden stars ...'

I swept the lot on to the floor and, though it was not yet six o'clock, reached for the whisky bottle.

I was late to school next day, of course, not really late but five minutes before the bell. The headmaster expected us there five minutes earlier than that, and would stand at the entrance frowning at late-comers. He frowned at me, and the fact that I was dabbing at a cut chin didn't help.

I hated this headmaster and I think I should explain why. His name—absurd name—was Carl Poling. He was not much older than me, and that was perhaps the first reason for the antipathy I felt: I resented that a man of my age, with no qualifications for the job and decided disadvantages of character, was in a position of authority over me. On top of this I had come across him earlier in my career. For three terms we had been in the same secondary modern in Camden Town where he had been in charge of Chemistry and I had not liked him then. He was tall, quite good-looking I suppose, and affected a goatee beard. In his early days he was 'chummy' (his word) with the pupils who quietly mocked his less prepossessing habits. He was known as the 'pocket billiards player' because he would stand in front of a class with one hand in his trouser pocket and fiddle with himself. However, he was a fixer. When, in his earlier days, he talked with a headmaster, a governor, or an inspector, he always said 'sir', just once, at the beginning of each conversation; he was deadly at personal P.R.—he got the school to the final of a T.V. competition for young scientists, and he went to conferences and never let a lecture go by without finding something to say in question time. He was, I gather, a lousy chemist, but he played snakes and ladders on the administrative side of the profession—the snake who got up all the ladders.

That morning I found in my pigeon-hole a slip from him saying that the money available for the English department in the financial year just starting was nine hundred and fifty pounds. This was a cut of five percent and I knew that the Local Education Authority had increased the overall allowance to the school by six percent. I had a free period later in the morning and I managed to catch the man in his office. To cut a long story short, I lost my temper and, no doubt because of the state I was in from the weekend, presented my case badly and probably cut a pretty sorry figure.

Another sore was touched during the day when a fifth former, quite a bright boy, said towards the end of a lesson that he was bored with *Romeo and Juliet*.

What was I doing teaching adolescents to be *bored* with *Romeo and Juliet*?

Make no mistake: he was not bored because I did not know how to present the play to him meaningfully. I am not a bad English teacher. But I had not done *Romeo and Juliet* with him. I had prepared him, laboriously and repetitively, over some months, to write in half an hour in the 'O' level exam a well-planned essay in answer to a question like 'Examine the contribution made to the play by the character of the Nurse'.

One good thing did happen that day. On the way home I had to do some shopping in town and coming out of Smith's I heard the transatlantic accents of Del Quay.

'Hey, Mr Elmer. Come and have a coffee with me.'

She led me down the road to the Wimpy Bar, planted herself opposite me and ordered coffees. I was excited. There she was—five feet two inches of vivacity with long chestnut hair, a plumpish face, wicked small brown eyes, and an intelligence as incisive as I've ever come across. Her father was an oil executive whose corporation was spending four years prospecting the Sussex coast line for oil, would you believe? They actually had a couple of wells bubbling up west of Brighton. He was a liberal sort of man who insisted that his extremely talented child should go to the local comprehensive and on to Southampton University. I had taught her for two years in the sixth form and she had gained a grade 'a' in English.

'How's Southampton?' I asked.

'Oh gee, great! Athens in the time of Pericles?' She dipped a finger in the froth of her coffee and sucked it provocatively. 'No, it's OK, I guess. I'm just bored with being educated.'

'You should have read English.'

She was doing combined honours—French and Spanish.

'Sure. But would I have found teachers like you?'

'Oh come off it, Del.'

'No, really, Mr Elmer. You were great. You made me think: no one else ever did. No, I guess English would have been pretty dull after you. I guess I just went to University too soon—I should have had a year off.' Suddenly she put on a husky Marlene-ish sort of voice. 'I need adventure.'

'We all do.'

'You find me adventure, Mr Elmer, and I'll do anything for you.' Same voice.

My heart gave a little jump—why not? She was much of an age with Jill.

'I just might, Del. I just might.'

I thought I was kidding.

The next day, Tuesday, I sneezed again, and again there was that card. This time it was the lunch hour and Saul was with me. He had hardly spoken to me on Monday—partly because our paths in that comprehensive factory of good citizens did not cross on Mondays; partly, I suspected, because I had not let him out of the back garden at the party. However, Tuesday lunchtimes we played bridge—the Head of Science, a German teacher who actually was German, Saul and I. We had just played an interesting hand. With eight points I had opened three spades, having eight of them to the King and the Queen of Hearts covered. Wilf, the German, was unable to resist a punitive double in spite of the convention he played with his partner. Saul passed, and Clive, the scientist, took the double as a serious bid and, having a poor hand and remembering the convention, bid four clubs. Wilf left him in it. Saul with Ace, Queen and two other clubs, doubled, and they were four down. The irony was that I would have made three spades anyway.*

As Wilf dealt I sneezed, and passed the Chichesters' card across to Saul.

'What do you make of that?' I asked.

Saul glanced at it before picking up his hand.

'Pot?' he said.

The hairs on my neck rose.

'I'll run you to the station tonight,' I said, 'but first we'll have a cup of tea at my flat.'

Saul came in behind me and stood a yard or so inside the living room, head pushed forward, nose poking this way and that, seeing what had changed since his last visit. He always does this. I went into the kitchen, plugged in the kettle, and fiddled with cups and so on. When I went back he was standing by the bookshelves looking at a recent purchase—*Eroticism in Western Art* by Lucie-

* Six spades, two clubs, and one heart.

Smith. He was making a sort of 'hee-hee' noise, another thing he often does. It irritated me: I wasn't sure whether he was going 'hee-hee' at the book or at the fact that I had bought it. I poured the tea.

'Why did you say "pot" when I showed you that card?'

'The Chichesters' card?' He thought for a moment. 'Silly of me really. I could get people into trouble like that.'

'Oh come on, Saul. Not through me you couldn't.'

'No, I suppose not.' He dunked a ginger nut and sucked it. 'Six or seven years ago when the cannabis thing first really got going, they were on the scene pushing it round the shoddy end of the theatre and telly. I don't think they recognised me, but I knew them. They've come on in the world a bit since then. But to me they still mean "pot".'

'They still do.'

'What?'

'Mean "pot".'

'Really? How do you know?'

I repeated to him most of what I could remember about the conversation. 'They said any respectable-looking ordinary person with a family could bring it in off the package tours and they told me I should have a family.'

'And they gave you that card?'

'No, I found it in my coat pocket in the morning.'

'Oh yes, and just where did you get to that morning?'

'Jill's.'

'Jill's?'

'That dark girl's flat.'

'Bloody marvellous! Quite the raver, aren't you?' He grinned broadly at me, leant back in the sofa and fished out a cigarette packet. 'They were trying to recruit you, you know.'

Suddenly I couldn't meet his eyes.

'Yes,' I said, 'that was what I was beginning to think.'

'And,' he added, with a note of amused certainty in his voice, 'you are interested.'

'Yes, I think I might be.' I stood up and walked round the room a bit and then stubbed out my cigarette. 'What do I do now?'

'What do you think the card's for?'

'Yes. Yes. Well, I'll take you to the station.'

He laughed and stood up.

At first the idea seemed quite attractive: it would be exciting, add a bit of spice to the summer, show there was life in the old dog yet. Then imagination took over. Think of the airport, the Customs, the long queues of sunburnt, hungover, irritable families and squalling children, clutching their souvenirs, cigarette packages and bottles of spirits, and me in the middle of it all with a suitcase of cannabis, ashen and shaking—I'd never be able to do it. And would it be worth it? Mike Chichester had said he made a thousand on one trip, add on what he had kept for himself, make it twelve hundred. What would he pay a courier? Certainly not more than half. I could not see myself risking imprisonment, fines, loss of job, and all the anxiety for less than three months' salary. I tried to put it out of my head and concentrate on school work.

I couldn't settle. I drank coffee, walked round the whisky bottle, played records. The thought of Jill kept coming back, just like a fever—sometimes with a feeling both euphoric and exciting, more often with a deep ache of longing. The memories that were now so intense would fade, soon I should find it difficult to remember her face; in a year's time I might pass her in the street without recognising her. I hurt myself hammering my fist on my work-desk at this thought. She had made me feel alive again, made my flat, my job, my broken marriage seem banal, dead. I wanted out—before it was too late. It was as if I were a prisoner in some awful dungeon, chained to the wall, and the jailer's daughter had slipped in one night and loosened the gyves: if I acted now I might escape; if I did not the jailer would discover the weak links and soon I would be as secure again as I had ever been.

Was smuggling pot to be the next step out of the dungeon? Well, not for a mere six hundred pounds, it wasn't.

'Mr Poling would like to see you. I think you're free second period, aren't you?' This was Chloë, the headmaster's secretary. Often she would smile at me in a faintly ironical way which used to disconcert me, but now she looked serious.

'Oh Lord, what now?' I asked. I was on my way in for the last time that term.

She shrugged. 'He doesn't tell me much.' This was something which still niggled her and was one of the reasons why she regretted the retirement of her previous boss and was looking for a post in another school.

At the end of the first period I went to the staff-room and smoked a slow cigarette—hoping I was keeping the man waiting. This worked better than I had expected. Just as I was reaching for an ashtray there was a bleep from the tannoy system and then, heard in about eighty classrooms, study areas, workshops, gyms, and offices. 'Mr Poling is waiting for Mr Elmer in Mr Poling's office.'

The tannoy was our Master's most irritating innovation.

Off I trotted, self-consciously aware of the mirth which nearly two thousand people would be sharing at my expense.

'Come in, Mark. Take a seat.' He was sitting behind his desk (his lamented predecessor had had a round table) but, as I sat down, he stood up, walked to the window and turned in front of it, hands in pockets, possibly fiddling with himself. At any rate he was now nicely silhouetted against the light. I'd been through this sort of thing before, but even so I felt a tightening of blood vessels. I wished I still had some of the Librium the doctor had prescribed during Poling's second term.

'I didn't bring this up yesterday, old boy, because you were already a bit upset over your share of the capitation. However, I know we now see eye to eye over that.' He moved to his desk and picked up a form. I recognised a requisition I had sent through the bursar.

'I see here you have ordered copies of *The Millstone* and *The Girl with Green Eyes.*'

'Yes. They are for the C.S.E. libraries.'

This was really Saul's pigeon. We were developing a course for children not good enough for 'O' level, and one important and very successful part of it was reading adult fiction—a break from the lighter classics or stories about children which are the traditional fare for such fifteen and sixteen-year-olds.

'Don't misunderstand me, Mark. Both novels doubtless have literary value. I am no judge of that. But I am concerned with the moral welfare of our customers.' He often referred to the children in this way. Now I saw that he had a copy of each book on his desk; he picked one up. '*The Millstone* tells the story of an unmarried mother; *The Girl with Green Eyes,* which features a nude on the cover, describes an adulterous affair between a teenager and a middle-aged man.'

I tried to be reasonable.

'We have had both in the school for a year. That

requisition is to make up numbers for next year's extra class. Both are very popular, especially with the girls...'

'My goodness, Mark. Do you know what you are saying?'

'...and as far as I know, the incidence of pregnancy among them was nil and I heard of no affairs with older men.'

'Mark, you will not be frivolous.'

'I have never been more serious; look...'

'I'm sorry.' He was now standing behind his desk, his face white, his fists clenched like a gorilla supporting itself uncertainly as it rose primordially to its hind feet. Evolution's mistake perhaps. 'I'm sorry. You will not order these books. You will withdraw the copies you have already from these class libraries. I repeat. My concern is the moral welfare of the children. I also have to consider what the parents of Ventleigh think of our school.'

I interrupted. 'The second I believe. If the first is true, God help the children of Ventleigh.'

And I got out.

I told Saul about it over coffee a few minutes later. He was as shocked as I was, but perhaps a shade more prepared to see some humour in it all.

'Have you done anything about the Chichesters?' he asked as we set off for our classrooms at the end of break.

I had forgotten all about them.

'No,' I said after a moment, 'I haven't. I don't see how they can pay more than five or six hundred pounds, and I should need a lot more than that if smuggling pot is to be my route out of here. No, I'll get a job in a College of Education.'

'Five or six hundred?' He stopped. 'Don't you ever read the papers?'

'Not all of them.'

'A couple got done in Lewes a couple of weeks ago. They

had forty thousand pounds' worth of hashish with them.'

'Forty thousand?' I am ashamed to say I could only manage a hoarse whisper.

'Think about it,' he said.

I thought about it. Forty thousand. But they had been caught. Done. Prison.

Christ!

CHAPTER IV

On the Wednesday evening then I rang up the Chichesters. As far as I remember the conversation went something like this.

'Could I speak to Mr Chichester, please?'

'Speaking.'

'Ah. I don't suppose you remember me. My name is Mark Elmer. We met last Saturday at that party in Putney.'

'Yes, yes, of course Mark, I do remember you.'

'And our conversation. About, er, package tours, and so on.'

'Yes.'

'You left your card in my jacket pocket.'

'Did I?'

This was turning out to be more difficult than I had expected.

'Well, I may have misunderstood you, but with one thing and another I thought you might be interested to know that I could be going on a package tour in August.'

'I see.'

There was a long pause which I was determined not to break. After all, I had made most of the running: it was up to him now.

'You must be starting your Easter holiday from school round about now,' he said at last.

'We finished school today.'

'Good.' And he rang off, just like that, leaving me puzzled and confused.

In the second post on Thursday there was a typed, unsigned note asking me to be in Kew Gardens, on the steps of the Palm House, at one o'clock on Friday.

I waited there for him for nearly twenty minutes—not an unpleasant spot on a blowy, sunny April morning with the cherry trees just coming in to bloom, and the huge fountain playing on the other side of the lake. I strolled up and down the narrow plaza in front of Decimus Burton's magnificent cast-iron and glass palace, and contrived not to feel too irritated at the banality of the Queen's Beasts that are set into the parapet. But I felt exposed: no doubt because I was being carefully watched. At last I turned at one end of the walk and coming back found him sitting on a bench at the other end as if he had been there all the time. He looked as smooth as ever, beautifully dressed in a creaseless dark suit, his black hair, thick and glossy, just curling over his collar, his skin tanned but just a shade sallower in the bright sunlight than I remembered. He was nursing a black and chrome attaché case on his knee.

'Mark Elmer, how nice to see you again.' He stood up and shook hands, and then guided me firmly by the elbow down the steps and right towards an area of hedges and lawns. We came to rest in an angle of thick yew hedges which sheltered a magnificent Weeping St Lucia Cherry, just bursting into luxuriant bloom.

'I don't think the grass is damp.' He stooped and touched it. 'No. Shall we sit down for a bit?'

There was a dream-like air of unreality about the whole situation, the two of us curtained by swathes of white flowers, leaning against the black, papery bark of the tree's

37

bole, the oily green of the hedges shutting us off from the rest of the world as if we were clandestine lovers. I could not suppress a shudder of apprehension.

He opened the attaché case and took out a neatly wrapped package.

'Sandwich?' he asked. 'Smoked salmon, I think. It's a pleasant spot for lunch, don't you agree?'

Mesmerised, I took a sandwich. It was smoked salmon. Vaguely I wondered if it was drugged.

We sat there for about three minutes eating sandwiches and saying absolutely nothing while the breeze tossed the mindblowing blossoms a few inches above our heads. At last I could bear it no longer.

'How much could I expect if I smuggled hashish into England for you?'

'Up to six years, I should think.' He smiled. 'I'm afraid I have nothing to drink and you look as if you could use one. Have an apple.'

'No thank you.' He had given me a fright and I had begun to dislike him.

'But you have brought up the topic and that is gratifying, though a shade indiscreet on your part. After all, one of us could be a policeman in the C.D.I.U. I have looked carefully into your background and I am sure that you are Mark Elmer, the same Mark Elmer that teaches at Ventleigh Comprehensive. Even so, it's just possible that you have been very recently recruited by the C.D.I.U., but unlikely, I think. The police do not like using irregulars unless they have to, and as far as I know they are doing quite well enough without them.'

'What, for heaven's sake, is the C.D.I.U.?'

'The Central Drugs Intelligence Unit. An entirely new arm of the Law.'

'I see.'

'Yes, well. I might as well warn you that they are on to me—which is one reason why we are meeting here and not at Twickenham, and why I did not arrange this rendezvous over the phone. I am fairly sure I am being tapped.'

I picked up the last quarter sandwich, and put it down again. The blossom shook and shivered above me and I felt unseen eyes peering at me through the yew hedge.

'How can you be sure you weren't followed here?' I asked.

Chichester swallowed the sandwich I had just put down —whole, I should imagine—and flicked crumbs from the corner of his mouth and jacket.

'If I had not learnt to spot a tail and shake him off years ago I should not still be in business.'

'Oh.'

There was another pause. I became conscious of the sounds around us—the rustle of the blossom the more distant susuration of the fountain on the lake, lost conversations, and a child laughing.

'At ten per cent of the retail value I should say not less than five thousand pounds and all expenses,' he said.

'What?'

'That's what you should get, if we are clever enough not to land in jail.' He stood up and dusted himself down. 'Are you still interested?'

I got up. 'Yes, of course.'

'Why?'

'Why not?' I couldn't think of anything else to say.

'Well. For five thousand pounds you risk—and it is a considerable risk, say one chance in five you will be caught —you risk your job, your career, respectability, several years' freedom. What do you earn at the moment? Three thousand a year? All right—for someone with your ability, qualifications, that is a nonsense. Nevertheless I am offering you less than twice that. I want to know why you are tempted.'

We had moved away from the St Lucia Cherry and he was walking me briskly along the back of the Palm House. At this point he stopped and fixed me with what, no doubt, he thought was a compelling eye. I think I faced it out rather well.

'My wife has left me—she was earning more than I and together we had a respectable income. Teaching bores me, sometimes disgusts me. Five thousand pounds is just about right—it will buy me two years, even three if I live carefully. In that time I think I might learn to write. Nothing grand you know—television perhaps, light novels, that sort of thing. But really I have reached a crisis and that's the sort of money I need to get me through.'

Obviously he was convinced. He slapped my shoulder and cried, 'Bravo, I think we're in business. Let's have a drink. In one of the pubs on the Green, I think. No, this way. Let's walk across the grass—still plenty of narcissi about and I can't bear the tulips and wallflowers they are planting out on the walks. So suburban.'

We drank behind the pub in a little garden with a dovecot. Dimly one was aware of the river on the other side of a thick hedge—elm as far as I remember. He had a brandy, I a lager.

'Basically the problem, Mark, the problem is that you don't have a family. You look right. You're the right age, but on your own the Customs would notice you almost as readily as if you were twenty years younger and your hair twenty inches longer. What I want is a man, with a wife, and preferably with two children. You can't manage that I suppose? I mean your wife won't rejoin you just for a fortnight in August?'

'No.' I tried to think of Doctor Helen Elmer smuggling hash. 'No, that's definitely not on.'

'Still not to worry, not necessarily. I tell you what. You've got three weeks' holiday now, lucky devil. All right, two and a bit. You go through all your acquaintance. Find some lady about your age, who'll come in with you and, if I like her, I'll fix you up with a joint passport and we'll go ahead.' He looked at his watch—a thick gold slab of a thing. 'Look, I must dash.' He knocked back the brandy. 'Mark, it's been great meeting you again. I'll be in touch. I'll ring you, don't ring me: the tapping, remember? In, let's say, ten days.' He pulled out a thin pocket diary and pencilled in a note. 'On Monday the twenty-third, Shakespeare's birthday, appropriate date for a teacher of English, eh? Meanwhile don't let I dare not wait upon the adage, or whatever: find the lady, old chap.'

CHAPTER V

It may seem odd, but the classes I most enjoyed teaching were the fourth and fifth year C.S.E. band—those who could read and write but were thought not sufficiently academic for 'O' level—the ones you may remember who were in danger of being corrupted by Margaret Drabble and Edna O'Brien. There was a frank openness about them that I liked, a hearty scorn for school and a real lust for the life of cafés, discos, motor bikes, birds, fellers, football and so on which was just beginning to open up for them as they found—either by sweated labour as weekend and holiday shelf-fillers in supermarkets, or by petty crime—reasonable sums of money in their pockets. In their lives the 'bundle' figured quite largely—a rare event, but one which always provoked enthusiastic analysis the day after, enthusiasm which could be channelled into 'creative' writing. A good bundle always ended with some-one being 'properly done over'.

The Sunday night following my chat with Chichester at Kew I was 'done over' and 'properly' too.

The flat I had stood over a row of shops with a concrete area at the back and garages. I rented one of the garages near the end. I had been out for a drink and was return-ing at about half past ten. As I drove off the street into the compound I noticed a couple of largish men hanging about on the corner and thought nothing of it—Ventleigh has had, according to its local paper, several cases of mugging, but not so many as all that, not enough to put one on one's guard. One still takes law and order in the streets for granted.

They were technically astute and quick.

As I came round my Mini, they filled the gap between me and the garage door. For less than a second I had time to feel a spasm of incredulous alarm, real fear, but they did not give me time to cry out. The first blow, and I suppose it was with that old-fashioned but effective weapon the knuckle-duster, was accurately placed in my solar plexus. From then on I could not raise a noise louder than a wheezy gasp.

I'm not too sure how they did what they did to me after that, but it showed continuing efficiency—it hurt, a lot, but, I discovered later, left me pretty much unmarked. The worst bruises were behind and must have been caused by falling against the car. They smashed something—a black-jack, fist, boot?—repeatedly into my testicles; they sought out agonising pressure points in my neck and over my kidneys; finally they both spat in my face.

Then one of them leaned over me and I could smell the piss-like smell of stale beer on his breath.

'Listen, Jack. My name's Charley, and this here is my mate Paco, and our governor, Mr Jones, sent us. And Mr Jones says we're to say to you, keep off of that Chichester. Keep away from him. Don't go nowhere near him never-more. Right? Now we're told to be sure you understand, so smack the floor with your hand twice if you know what we mean. No more to do with that Mr Chichester, right?'

He was holding a large fist under my nose. In the light from the street which passed under the car I could see a heavy gold ring, carved like a skull. His face was in dark-ness.

I smacked the concrete floor, twice.

It must have been several minutes before I was on my feet. At the knee stage I vomited. Just then a neighbour's car drove into the garage next door but one to mine. The lights swung big black shadows around me but they did not see me. Why didn't I cry out, call to them for help? Because it was too late, my attackers had gone; because the only way of getting on their track would have involved telling the police the whole story; because I felt too tired to explain; because I was ashamed that anybody should see me in the state I was in.

When the yard was clear again I dragged myself up to my flat. I lay on the sofa for a bit and cried. Then I cleaned myself up and went to bed.

The following days did nothing to lessen my resolve: nothing would possibly induce me to see or speak to Chichester again. I admit to a mild curiosity about my attackers—they were young, I think I can say that, and Charley had fair hair. It disturbed me that they were young: it can't have been long since they were C.S.E. kids and I wondered if they were Ventleigh boys or if they had come down from London. I assumed that 'Mr Jones' was a business rival of Chichester's: it made Chichester's boast about shaking off a tail sound a bit sick. But whatever else I felt, I was sure that I had touched briefly a hellish world of violence and nastiness, and that one taste of it was enough. I did nothing about finding the wife Chichester wanted for me.

On the twenty-third of April I would have said that my determination was just as strong, but as the day wore on and Chichester did not ring I began to feel a little disappointed—a touch of chagrin. Apart from anything else I had planned various ways of answering him, my favourite being, 'Mr Elmer's residence, Chief Inspector Barlow of the Yard speaking.' But he did not ring, and I tried to forget about the whole business.

I even tried to get myself into something like a proper frame of mind for the beginning of the school term which was on the following Monday. By the Friday I was feeling very sick, heavily sick at the thought of the thirteen week Summer term through blazing June and July to holidays in wet or sultry August. I find it difficult to explain or describe the leaden feeling of dull despair that afflicted me again as I thought of *Coriolanus* and hundreds, and I mean hundreds on hundreds of compositions to mark, stretching ahead not just through the summer but through the next twenty-two years. And then, on Friday the phone rang. It was a woman, a bright cheerful voice, but not a youngster.

'Mark Elmer? It's you? Oh, I'm so glad I've been able to track you down. Look, I don't suppose you remember me, but the name's Joselinda Tangmere and we met at that ghastly party of the Slindons about three weeks ago. Well, actually it wasn't all that ghastly, was it? Well look. I've been asked to do an article on what comprehensive schooling means to the ordinary high street mum—you know the sort of thing—and I wondered, it just occurred to me, that perhaps you might let me pick your brains. Actually, I'm not too sure what a comprehensive school is, you know?'

I told her I should be happy to help her in any way she could suggest.

'Would you? Really? Oh, that is sweet of you. Look Mark, this may seem a bit much, but do say if it is. Could you possibly pop up to town tomorrow and call on me for lunch, and then we could have a nice tête-á-tête about schools and, oh, everything, in the afternoon. Is it awful of me to suggest that? Or are you too dreadfully busy just before term starts?'

45

Well, I've explained how I felt about term starting, and even as I mumbled out acceptance of her invitation I was imagining the avocado, the veal escalope, the soufflé, the coffee and cognac, and then the afternoon alone with a mature, experienced woman...

It wasn't a bit like that.

The weather had changed and it was one of those bleak, grey, weepy days when all the vegetation seems heavy and dripping and puddles begin to collect even in lawns. Not that Jo's house had a lawn: the grass hadn't been cut for months. I rang the bell at half past twelve and she opened the door dressed in jeans, a jumper, and a sloppy cardigan with an end of unwinding wool at the cuff. She had a cloth in her hand and her welcome seemed strained and nervous after her confident effusiveness on the phone. Weeks later she told me what an ordeal that call had been for her.

'Oh, here you are,' she said, and she glanced uneasily over my shoulder into the grey street as if to see if I had been followed. 'Look you'll have to excuse my appearance, but it is a bit silly, don't you think, to dress up in all one's finery and then mess about in the kitchen? Come on in, get that wet coat off, and have a drink.'

She showed me into a large front room which had once been well and expensively furnished. But the egg-shell white surfaces were scuffed and scratched; the fine mushroom carpet was stained and a bearskin rug shed its hair beneath a low-hanging globular lamp-shade which was shedding its raffia.

'Help yourself. There's gin and tonic, or whisky, and I think there's some quite good sherry left. But if there is, be careful, it's been open for simply ages. I'll be with you in a minute.'

I poured myself a gin and tonic and looked round hope-

46

fully for ice and lemon but couldn't find either. I sat down on a low leather armchair, one of those that feel spongy, lit a cigarette and took a long drink. I had mixed it strong and I began to feel better. Five minutes later Jo returned. She had put on some lipstick, taken off the cardigan and put on a gold chain necklace and a couple of large rings. I don't know that she was much improved.

'There, at last,' she said. 'Lunch ought to be all right for ten minutes or so. What are you drinking—gin and tonic? Lovely. Could you mix me one?'

I did and she fumbled around for her Gauloise. I lit it.

'That was how we met, wasn't it?' she said. 'Silly me, I can never find my lighter.'

She took a long drink, and I noticed that her hand was shaking quite a lot.

'Oh dear,' she said. Then she set down her drink and leant forward putting her elbows on her knees. She pushed her thin fingers with their long chipped nails across her temples and through her straw-coloured hair, and then shook her head.

'I'm sorry,' she said, and again she would not look at me. 'But I think I had better come straight to the point. Have you found the wife Mike Chichester wanted you to have?'

'No...' I was so surprised I could hardly think. 'But I didn't try. You see...'

She rushed on.

'He didn't think you would have done. Well. He thinks we could do it if I was your wife. I mean, he could get us a joint passport.'

Suddenly she looked straight at me.

'What do you think?' she asked. 'Of course, it would be less trouble for him if we got married.'

CHAPTER VI

'I'm having nothing to do ever with Mike Chichester.'

And I told her about how I had been beaten up.

'Oh, but that's awful,' she cried, when I had finished, putting a long drawn-out sliding note on the 'aw' of 'awful'. 'You poor dear, how truly dreadful.' She went on about it for a bit, then smoothed her hands down over her jeans and stood up.

'I suppose that's it then. I'm sorry I dragged you up here for nothing. But you might just as well stay and have some lunch. I'll just go and see to finishing it off. Do have another drink. I'll call you when it's ready.'

I poured myself another and sat down in the low chair again and tried to collect my thoughts. What an extraordinary thing—a proposal of marriage, no less. I looked around: Jo would be an even worse housekeeper than Helen had been, and sluttish with it. But then it wasn't on, anyway—I didn't think that even with the new laws we could get a divorce through by the summer. What an outrageous idea! Chichester certainly had a nerve. I jumped up and moved round the room feeling an odd sort of excitement—almost as if I had won a prize. Chichester really did seem to think I could make a go of it. But then the memory of the thugs in the garage, of pain so acute that I sweated even at the thought of it, came flooding back and I sat down again. No, under no circumstances would I ever do anything to risk a recurrence of that experience. Never. Still it had been a surprise, and now the day looked like being a real disappointment. I had already abandoned most of my fantasies about afternoon sex after being wined and dined, but I had looked forward to filling Jo in on comprehensives. I had planned to be quite amusing about them.

She had been away a long time. I looked at my watch— ten minutes, perhaps fifteen. Surely longer than 'finishing off' implied. I waited a moment or two more then poked my head into the hall. I could smell burning.

In the kitchen Jo was standing over a frying pan in which two slabs of meat were slowly blackening in a haze of smoke. Listlessly she pushed them to and fro with a fish-slice and tears ran down her cheeks. I hardly had time to take in the steamed-up windows, dirty cloths, grimy kitchen-ware before she dropped pan and slice and turned to me, almost falling against me and pushing me on to the sink. With the top of her head in my nose and her hot sobs heaving into my neck, I found some difficulty in groping a hand out to the stove to turn off the gas.

After a time her sobs became articulate—a steady stream of four-letter words interspersed with an occasional milder 'bloody hell' and the like. I managed to get her back to the living room, sat her down, lit her a Gauloise, and refilled her drink. At last she could speak properly.

'What a bloody silly sloppy cunt you must think me,' she gasped. 'I'm so sorry, but this really was to be my chance, perhaps the last.'

And then the story came out. Two years before she had been charged and fined for being in possession of cannabis; her husband had left her, and because of the quality of the life she had been living, he won custody of the two children. Under the financial settlement he had paid up all outstanding bills and left her the house with a small mortgage, but this had not worried her then—her journalism had been doing very well indeed. But a lean period had followed: she drank more, ran up bills, let the house fall into disrepair, and editors had just not wanted to know; she was at the end of her tether. Then along came Chichester with his fantastic proposition and it seemed like a gift from heaven.

'Don't you see?' she concluded. 'The money would just about clear up all I owe including the mortgage. I could really settle down and try to live decently. Without debts, I could try to get some simple, unglamorous, steady job, and perhaps the court order on the children would be reversed. The judge said it could be reviewed at a later date. And then this happens, and you can't do it, and I don't blame you ...' She began to cry again.

I poured some more gin and found tonics to go with it in the fridge in the kitchen. When I got back she seemed to have a grip on herself again.

'Would you like a snack at a pub?' I suggested.

'No. No, I'm not hungry. But would you stay here with me for a bit, and talk? It's going to be awfully lonely after you've gone. Tell me a bit about yourself.'

Well, I suppose it was the drink, and what is called 'the emotionally charged atmosphere', but I let go a bit too about how the quality of my life left much to be desired and how Chichester's offer had seemed a way out for me also. Then after another gin or two she moved down on to the hairy rug at my feet and began cuddling my knees while I ran a tentative finger through her hair. The gas-fire in front of us helped to create an increasingly cosy feeling and I began to feel quite, you know, excited. But then she started crying again.

'Look,' I said, 'why can't Chichester find someone else

50

to go with you? It doesn't have to be me.'

'Yes, it does,' she sobbed.

'Why?'

'Because he's already got other couples doing it. Normally he doesn't approach single people; it was only because he thought you wouldn't find anyone that he came round and asked me...' She started crying again and I realised that I was beginning to feel really sorry for her. The drink I suppose.

Suddenly she twisted round to face me.

'You know, no one need know at all, if we did it.'

'What do you mean?' I asked. 'Do what?' I wondered hazily to myself.

'Went through with Chichester's plan.'

'I should hope not.' For a moment I felt pettish.

'No, don't be stupid. I mean the man who employed those thugs. The mysterious Mr Jones. We could arrange it all without you meeting Chichester again. I'll explain to him why you don't want to see him. We can probably fix it so that not even I ever actually see him. If we do that, then how are these other people going to know at all?'

I thought about it for a moment, trying to make my brain clear.

'Did Chichesh ... did he tell you what the plan was?'

'In outline, yes. It's very simple.' She gulped, made an effort, and began to talk in a simple almost childish way, like a tearful girl explaining a problem. 'As a married, respectable, middle-class couple we're packed off on a package tour to Morocco at the height of the season. The hotel will be a good one and we do just the things most tourists of a very ordinary sort do. On our last night, while we are having dinner, all our belongings will be removed and our luggage filled with hashish. We go through Customs in the normal way, the flight has been carefully chosen to coincide with a really busy, congested time at Gatwick, and once we're through he's there to meet us, take the cases, and pay us off.'

'Pay us off. Yes. How much?'

She looked up at me sharply.

'One hundred pounds a kilo is what he first offered. But I know the price he'll get for it on the market—more than a thousand pounds a kilo, and if he can get it on to the States he'll get twice that again. So I got him up to three hundred pounds a kilo.'

'How much will that come to? I'm not very good with kilos.'

'Well, the normal luggage allowance for a package holiday is fifteen kilos per person. If we use all, or nearly all of that, it makes four thousand five hundred pounds each.'

The room suddenly felt very hot and stuffy. I took another pull at the tepid gin and tonic and the numbers whirled, danced, and stumbled in my mind.

'Over a thousand a kilo. Perhaps say twelve hundred. Thirty times twelve. Um, twelve times thirty, twenty-four, thirty-six thousand pounds. I'd do it for that. Yes, I'd do it for that, or a good half share of that even.'

She was looking bewildered. 'What are you on about?' she asked.

I grinned at her. Probably rather sloppily.

'You didn't think, did you,' I burbled, 'that I ever even contemplated doing it for a few measly thou, a pittance. That! for Chicheshtersh pittance. I'll do it for *all* the money, though. If you'll help me.'

She looked at me as if I was mad.

'How?' she asked, at last.

Not very coherently, I told her.

Part Two

CHAPTER I

Chichester's instructions had been very explicit. We were
to spend a fortnight in the Aladdin Palace on the Atlantic
coast six kilometres from Tangiers. On our last night we
were to pack everything that we were prepared to 'lose'
in the two large suitcases. What we wanted to keep—night
things, toiletries and so on, together with a small number
of gifts, souvenirs and the like, were to be left in the
bathroom. These we would carry through Gatwick in
peasant-weave camel bags together with all the ordinary,
dutiable stuff within the allowances. Chichester was very
firm (so Jo told me, for I stuck to my self-imposed rule
of never going near him) that we should not exceed our
allowances. If we did and the Customs spotted it then they
would go through the lot. And that would mean thou-
sands of pounds in fines, and jail, for during our last
evening meal the two suitcases would have been emptied
and repacked with thirty kilos of first quality hashish.
Chichester would pay the fines, she said, but about prison
sentences he would be able to do nothing.

The Aladdin was a very pleasant hotel and Jo and I
really had quite a nice time there. I suppose it's fairly
common to sneer at this sort of holiday but I found nothing to grumble at: the rooms were well-appointed, the ser-
vice was excellent, the food good and varied. There were

swimming pools, lessons in water-skiing and schnorkelling; one could go riding, play tennis and I don't know what all. There were coach trips into the mountains and guided tours of the old town.

My relationship with Jo had quickly settled into an uncomplicated pattern—almost from the moment, way back in April, when we decided to go through with it. Really we were rather dissimilar in tastes and background and, by tacit agreement, we remained a business partnership—on entirely friendly terms you understand, but without anything deeper at all: no sex in other words. Well, that's not quite true. On our second night sharing a room at the Aladdin we both got a bit drunk and, stumbling into the room, giggling a lot, fell on to one of the twin beds and tried fumblingly and unsuccessfully to fuck. When this proved to be beyond us Jo threatened to spank me with her hairbrush and—one thing led to another. All this was pleasant and we tried similar activities on several more occasions during our stay. So—a little sex, yes. But no passion. Which made her subsequent behaviour all the more surprising. But, as they used to say in the books I read as a child, I anticipate.

As the fortnight wore on we both began to feel the strain, but anticipation made us more light-headed than soberly anxious. I think this was because the risks that were looming up over us were to be our risks, not taken on behalf of Chichester. It was beginning to feel, at least in part, a bit of a joke. So much so that, as we reached the fruit stage of our last meal on the terrace of the Aladdin the urge to rush up to our room and see what was going on there became almost irresistible.

'It's a bit like Christmas,' I suggested. Jo leaned forward. She was wearing a low-cut silk blouse in a trendy print, and a long skirt. In that light, with the warmth of the night air, the odours of Arab spices, the crickets, and the steady roar of the ocean, she looked quite delectable for all that she was over forty. That had come out over the passport bit—Chichester had insisted that the information on the phoney document we shared should be as accurate as possible.

'Whatever made you say that?' she asked.

'Father Christmas is e'en now putting our presents in our room.' I'm afraid I'm a little given to expressions like 'e'en now' when I'm excited or tipsy. The pedagogue wasn't quite yet dead in me. 'I want to go and have a look.'

'You mustn't,' she whispered, and then giggled behind her hand. 'Let's!'

It was my turn to feel nervous, since she was now egging me on.

'Madame, we shall exercise due restraint in this as in everything. Chichester would not want us to show unusual haste. Would Madame like an oriental coffee? Madame would? Ahmet!'

'How do you know his name is Ahmet?'

'Of course it is. See, he's coming.'

Twenty minutes later we made it upstairs. The suitcases had been filled with packages about the size of an ordinary brick, wrapped and hermetically sealed in gleaming, heavy foil.

We gazed at them for a moment.

'Phew,' I said. 'Chichester's organisation works all right. Let's hope ours does.'

Jo squeezed my hand.

'Just about a thousand pounds a kilo,' she murmured.

The very first hint that we had to show that our organisation was up to his did not come until the coach cruised past the airport car-park. Briefly we caught a glimpse of the two Volkswagen vans, one orange and white, one dark blue, parked up against the fence as near to the departure areas as possible. I could not restrain myself.

'They're here,' I hissed.

'I know. They had to be.' She looked very pale and I could see a pulse throbbing in her neck.

My throat was dry. 'Right,' I croaked. 'Here we go.'

Actually it worked perfectly, without a hitch.

Our two suitcases were hauled with the rest of the tour's luggage out of the coach's trunk and wheeled into the departure area where they were dumped near the counter of the tour operator. His name really was Ahmet and he was half Arab, a quarter French and a quarter American. I had spent a pleasant and fruitful hour with him in the airport cafeteria the previous morning. I nodded to him and he nodded back. That nod had been paid for in advance—fifty pounds plus what he could make on our unused air tickets.

A crowd of fellow travellers, many of whom had been at our hotel, were milling around in the confused anxious way people have at such times—trying to check that their luggage had been unloaded from the coach, uncertain whether they were responsible for it now, losing their children, fumbling for passports, and so on. I had a moment's anxiety, and then I saw them—Saul and Del Quay. Saul was in a khaki shirt and denims and a ridiculous Australian-type bush hat which, perched above his too long hair, made him look like General Custer in *Little Big Man*. I was faintly pleased to see that his nose was peeling. Del Quay looked fabulous in a flowery loose blouse or smock and white jeans. I caught her eye. She grinned and gave a characteristic flip to her long chestnut hair to get it back over her shoulder. For three years I had found this mannerism exciting—ever since she joined my 'A' level English group.

They pushed through the crowd towards us, stopping once to detach a four-year-old lolly-sucking kid who, having lost his real dad, wanted Saul.

'Everything is OK,' I said, and without wasting any more time Saul and I each picked out of the luggage one large olive green leather suitcase and marched, in file, back through the waiting area, out from under the canopy that sheltered the concourse, and into the blazing heat of the Moroccan sunlight. As we struggled along through the heat towards the car-park a Boeing 707 roared off a nearby runway, its gleaming silver nose thrusting up into the deep blue and its cloud of black haze spilling out behind. I glanced back to see how the weaker sex were coping. Jo looked a bit grumpy, perhaps because she was now stuck with four camel bags, out of one of which poked the plastic top of a hideous hookah thing she had bought in the *souk*. Del said something to her and Jo nodded, but the words were drowned in the scream of another jet.

We made it to the vans and, still without saying much, loaded the cases into the orange and white one. Jo and I climbed in, Saul slammed the door beside me and gave a thumbs-up sign.

'See you in Málaga,' he said, and sauntered off to the blue van. Del blew me a kiss, trotted a step or two to catch him up and took his hand. Bloody hell, I thought.

'So far so good,' I said aloud. I wiped my wet palms on my trousers, turned the ignition key, and waited for Saul to lead us down to the port. 'All right?'

'Fine,' said Jo.

'They seem to have managed very well. They even look fit on it.'

'Yes. Del said she thought you were looking well.'

'Yes. Well, I expect I am. Here we go.'

'Remember. Drive on the right.'

'On the right. Yes.'

We had a bad fright at the car-ferry terminal when the Customs waved a Saab out of the queue about six places in front of us. We could see the consternation on the Swede's face, and the firmness with which the Arab officials ignored him as they began unloading his boot. It had not seemed possible to us that this could happen—a Customs check on leaving a country. We would be sunk if they picked on us. It would be almost as disastrous if they picked on Saul since it would take him out of his place in front of us. With pulse rate up and a nasty, bitter taste in my mouth I waited for his turn. But no: they waved him on. Jo wound down her window.

'*Pasaportes.*' The brown face of an official, the thin, silky, black moustache, the gleam of gold in his teeth. '*Inglés.* Eeenglish. Verrry gooood.' He poked his head in. A stream of Arabic followed. We looked helplessly at each other and then back at him.

'*¿No comprende?*' he asked, and grinned. 'Much luggage, many souvenirs.' He plucked Jo's blasted hookah out of the bag which she was now carrying on her lap. The rubber hose thing flapped about and banged the mouthpiece on the door stanchion. 'Puff, puff. Verrrry gooood. OK, Eeenglish, have a safe voyage.'

'Oh Christ,' said Jo, as fumblingly she pushed the hookah back into the bag. 'If every Customs post is going to be like this I shall die of fright long before we get home.'

We had decided to avoid each other on the ferry—we calculated that the feeling of relief would be so great as the boat sailed that there would be a real possibility of making fools of ourselves or even saying something indiscreet and loud enough to give the show away. So Jo and I found a cool lounge in the front of the ship and settled down to *Cuba Libres* and the excitement of seeing Tangiers, burning white in the sunlight, slipping away to starboard.

However, it's a five-hour trip to Málaga and one can drink a lot of rum and Coke in that time. Jo began to feel sleepy after an hour or so and, feeling the need for fresh air, I left her to doze.

The deck was a bracing world of white and blue which lifted my spirits immediately. I suppose reaction after the anxiety of meeting Saul and Del and getting the hash on board had left me feeling depressed. But outside everything was grand. There was a fine stiff breeze and the boat cut a swath of the purest whiteness out of the ultramarine of the sea; gulls, almost as white, wheeled and flashed against the cobalt sky, or swooped behind the flagpole where the red and gold ensign of Spain jerked above our wake. On the port bow the hump of Gibraltar was already visible in a lilac haze and to the right the African coast was still near enough to make out white villages with red roofs, minarets and palm trees, and the Atlas mountains brooding titanically in the distance.

'Isn't this just great? I mean, really?'

Del was at my elbow; the breeze was blowing her hair about her mouth and her thin blouse against her small beautiful breasts. She never wore a bra. Her eyes were shining and she was obviously very excited.

'Hey, you oughtn't to be here. We're not meant to see each other yet.'

'Oh come on. This is a classless ship; you can't turn me off the deck.'

61

Indeed I could not.

'Besides, where's the harm of an Englishman and an American girl having a casual chat about their trips when they meet?'

'OK, all right, then. This is just great, like you said.'

'You always taught me to say "as" in that sort of sentence. Have you no respect for your mother tongue?'

Suddenly I felt really happy, exultant. I was suspended between two continents, in possession of at least thirty-six thousand pounds' worth of goods, slightly drunk, and the fabulous Del Quay was flirting with me.

'How's Saul?' was all I could think of saying.

'Saul's fine. He's a bit of a drag sometimes—all the way down he called the French "froggies" and the Spanish "dagoes" and we've been eating baked beans and canned ground beef stew all the time. No, you call it minced. Do you know what canned English minced beef stew is like? Ugh. But he's OK.'

I wanted to ask if they'd been making love at nights.

'Where is he now?'

'Getting plastered in one of the bars.'

'He'd better not get too drunk.'

'Why not? He reckons if he's obviously tight when we land then we're bound to be busted. He's full of ideas: another is that we should be smoking home-rolled cigarettes made to look like joints.'

'Did you see either of the others?' asked Jo when I got back to the lounge.

'I happened to bump into Del,' I answered, casually.

Jo was looking puffy and blotched, her cheek creased from the pressure of the mock leather of the chair she had dozed off in.

'I thought perhaps you might,' she said, and then went

on through a yawn, 'I hope you haven't bitched it all up through doing that.'

I felt niggled, almost angry—perhaps the strongest emotion Jo had yet produced in me.

Later, as we got nearer Málaga, she made me go to the gents and spruce myself up a bit; our plan depended to some extent on our appearance: while Del and Saul were to look as disreputable as they wanted, we had to look dull and respectable. Jo had certainly contrived the right effect—in a floppy cotton print dress down to her knees, and with the yellowy-brown skin of her tight little calves, and her slightly misshapen toes in thong sandals, she looked dowdy enough to be a curate's wife, let alone a teacher's.

CHAPTER II

Saul got busted all right. He is very irritating when he is drunk: he giggles a lot, sways about more than he really need, and worst of all, gives the impression that he is untouchably superior to anyone near him. He got the blue van off the boat in front of us all right, but as the guardias flagged him down I thought for a moment that he wasn't going to stop. At the last second he stood on everything.

First there were two in green uniforms with peaked caps, then some in grey, and finally a pair in those patent leather hats. Some Spaniards behind us began hooting. At last the van was waved over to the side and we were moved on. The one remaining official not involved with Saul glanced briefly at our passports, but his attention wasn't on us at all. Saul was now out on the tarmac and gesticulating with his hands above his head and his bush-whacker's hat pushed back above his florid face and mauve spectacles. Then Del climbed down and our policeman almost deserted his post.

'*Inglés. Muy bien*,' he said. And we were through.

It seems ridiculous: we thought we had covered every possible contingency and many wildly improbable ones in our plans—we ignored the blatantly obvious. Some-how it had seemed, as I enacted what would happen in my mind, that Saul and Del, having attracted attention to themselves, would quickly demonstrate their lack of illegal or dutiable goods and follow us out almost straight away. If I had thought about it at all it was simply in terms of pulling over to the roadside once we were through the customs and waiting for perhaps ten minutes. But even that would have been impossible. There were 'no parking' signs all the way down the avenue that led us round the port and out on to the Paseo del Parque and then, before we knew what was happening or where we were going, I was faced with five possible routes and a policeman on point duty who was getting increasingly impatient with my indecision.

'Go on,' shouted Jo.

'I can't,' I yelled back.

The policeman blew his whistle and began making those very brisk, masterful gestures Spanish cops reserve for idiot foreigners.

'You must.'

'I can't: once we're up in the town Saul will never find us.'

'I know, but you'll have to. For Christ's sake move.'

The policeman blew his whistle very hard and imperiously halted with magnificent confidence, street by street, all the traffic approaching the intersection. Then he let his whistle drop from his mouth to swing from its lanyard and, hitching his gun-belt, marched up to us.

'*Inglés*,' I stammered. '*No habla español*.'

'*¿Dónde puedo estacionarme?*' Jo tried, with far more sense and the Hugo phrase book.

There followed a lot more Spanish, a lot more of those firm chopping gestures; he went back to his podium, waved me up to him in a way that could not be denied, and directed me off down the side of the park. Then he blew his whistle and continued the interrupted orchestration of Málaga's traffic.

'Where are we going? What did you ask him?'

'I don't know where we are going. I asked him where we could park.'

Up above us, beyond palms and exotic plants, the cathedral floated.

'Look, this is impossible. We're getting further and further from the port. I'll have to turn and go back.'

'Oh Christ, Mark. One more bitch-up like the last, and he'll have us over to the nearest police station and the chances are they'll go through—*drive on the right* ... !' and she burst into hysterical sobs.

I had tried to go round a triangle of palms to get us back facing the port and, as I find often happens when driving on the wrong side of the road, the roundabout situation had taken me by surprise. Well, I sorted that out, quite well I thought, and there we were heading back past that very beautiful tropical park on one side and a whole lot of big buildings on the other. One had a balcony and was marked in large letters *Goberna Civil* or something like it which looked ominous. High on a hill, spectacularly sited, was the mediaeval castle: I wondered if they still used the dungeons.

Our policeman took it very well. His whistle dropped from his mouth again, and he looked as if he was going to explode, but this time I kept my head and drove on. He shrugged and let me pass.

'Quick, (sob), over there to the right, (sob).'

'What?'

'The bull ring.'

'Oh yes.' Mildly interested.

'You bloody oaf. There'll be parking space there.'

66

'Oh yes.' Understanding now.

There was of course lots of room all round the bull ring and I was able to choose a spot quite conspicuously close to the road from the ferry. If Saul didn't see us, we'd see him. That is, if he wasn't out already.

'Why didn't the policeman send us here?' I asked.

'We'd come from this direction, hadn't we? And it's not a very prepossessing area, is it?'

'I suppose that's so. Are you all right now?'

'Just. But Mark, please, please don't do things to attract the police's attention to us.'

'No. Of course not. I'll try not to.'

I lit a cigarette.

'How long are we waiting here?' she asked.

'Till they come out.'

'If they're not out already.'

'Quite.'

'Well don't you think we'd better go and see?'

'All right. You wait here . . .'

'Oh no. I'm not staying here on my own. Not with these suitcases.'

'But supposing he comes out . . .'

'Then he's bound to see us, isn't he? There's only one road away from the ferry.'

So down we both got and I locked up the van. Suddenly it seemed very hot. I suppose it was only about half a mile back to the Customs sheds and the surroundings were very picturesque—one could almost say beautiful—with the port shimmering in the afternoon sunlight, the palms, the cathedral, and the castle. I like ports, and this one had everything: yachts, sailing boats, pleasure craft as well as freighters, the car ferries and high-prowed Arab coasters. But by now the excitements of the day were taking their toll. I felt sick, my feet hurt, and I had a foul headache. I don't suppose Jo felt any better.

The police on duty at the various barriers on the approaches to the ferry terminal looked at us with curiosity but no one challenged us. Soon we were in the airy hangar where we had last seen Saul. It was almost deserted now, but over on one side the blue van was still parked. It had been jacked up at both ends and the wheels had gone. Del was standing nearby and there were three or four men around—one nosing in the rear-mounted engine, another two levering up the floorboards, a fourth carefully and destructively feeling his way through the upholstery of one of the two seats. There was no sign of Saul.

'Jesus, am I glad to see you,' said Del.

'What happened?'

'What do you think happened? It all worked just a sight too well.'

'Don't say things like that,' cried Jo. 'Don't talk about things working.'

'No. OK. Well,' Del spoke with heavily laboured phrasing, 'for some reason or other the fuzz decided that we looked like possible hash smugglers.' She went on more normally. 'And Saul was pissed and abusive. Whatever else happens, they'll probably bust him for drunk in charge. They've taken him away for a body search and probably it will be my turn after. If it's anything like what the pigs did to me once at J.F.K. airport, I'll learn to live with it. Mind you, I shan't like it, but I'll survive.'

'How long do you think you'll be?'

'For Christ's sake, how the hell do I know? It's going to take an hour anyway to put this lot back together,' she waved at the van, 'but personally I think it will depend on whether they give Saul a straight six months or the option of a fine. Which you'll have to pay.'

'Oh, quite.'

There was a long uneasy silence punctuated by the rhythmic tapping of a hammer on the chassis. Apparently there was another policeman we hadn't noticed under the van.

'I don't think we ought to stay here,' said Jo at last.

'Why ever not?'

'Well, I don't think we want to seem too closely connected to Saul and Del. When they find they're clean they might just decide to look us over after all.'

'Yes. You're right. Look Del...'

'So you're chickening out. Great. We'll see you sometime. Don't know where, don't know when...'

I realised Del was going to cry. Though I found this more touching than Jo's earlier outburst, I still couldn't help feeling that a shipload of monkeys would have been easier to manage than two females both hysterical together.

'Now calm down. Get a grip on yourself.' I tried to make my voice as calm and reassuring as I could. 'Look. We're parked in the parking lot outside the bull ring. It's at the end of the road from here. You can't possibly miss us.'

Jo interrupted.

'Look Mark. It could be tomorrow or the day after before we know what's happening. That car-park is not a camp site. You know the Spanish law on camping—there are tens of camp sites near Málaga, we're bound to be moved on...'

'All right. Point taken. Listen Del,' I squeezed her shoulder, paternally. So soft and delicate. 'We'll sit there till seven o'clock say, and then we'll go and find a pension. When we have I'll come back and leave a note under the windscreen wiper saying where we are. That way we'll meet you and Saul either at the pension or in the car-park

—we can't miss. OK? Plaza de Toros—bull ring. You've got that?'

'I suppose so. I wish you didn't sound like a school teacher.'

'You're a great girl. You really are.'

'Am I?'

'Sure thing.'

Jo interrupted again.

'For Christ's sake, come on.'

Jo and I spent an uncomfortable night in a cheap pension. We bickered almost all the time and it was far too hot and noisy to sleep. Back in the Plaza de Toros in the morning there was no sign at all of Saul and Del. We argued spasmodically and inconclusively throughout the morning about whether we should try to find out what had happened to them. Two o'clock came—siesta time. No hope of anything now before half past four, and the heat was unbearable. We went off and had a really foul paella in a cheap restaurant—all chicken claws and unidentifiable bits, vaguely marine in character, and cloggy, oily tepid rice.

Still no sign of them when we got back. I opened up all the doors and windows of the van in an attempt to make the temperature bearable, stumbling over the green suitcases as I did so. They were on the floor between the bench seats in the back. Jo sat in the wide side door fanning herself; then stretched back to get a drink from the cold box. We had stocked up on our way from the pension in the morning.

'Hey! Mark. Come and see.'

'What's the matter?'

'This case. It's been moved.'

I climbed out of the driver's seat and joined her.

'No. It's exactly where it was.'

'Of course it is. But it's the other way round. The Aladdin label was at the other end. And a corner has been torn. No, it's not the case that's different: someone has moved the label.'

'Don't be absurd. Why would anyone do a thing like that? Anyway the van's been all locked up, and none of the locks have been tampered with, I can promise you. You're imagining things.'

It was obvious to me that the strain we were under was aggravating her deeply-rooted anxiety neurosis. Her behaviour in the next few days bore out this diagnosis.

I was wondering whether opening the cases would calm her and I had just found the keys when there was a familiar sound of a V.W. engine and a crunch of gravel. Saul and Del had rejoined us.

They were in a foul temper. Saul had been fined two thousand pesetas, which I immediately reimbursed him, but the humility and sheer frustrating boredom of their experience had left a more lasting mark.

'What do you want to do now?' I asked.

Saul was firm.

'Just let's get going. The quicker we get back to England and through with this barmy business, the better. How far can we get tonight?'

'Granada?' I suggested. 'It's only about eighty miles but the roads are mountainous. There's a good camp site about six miles to the north of the town on the Madrid road.'

'OK,' said Saul. 'Granada or bust. Come on Del.'

As quickly as I could, I packed the suitcase keys away again at the bottom of my duffle bag. The idea of this was to create boredom in the mind of any Customs officer who might ask to see in the cases: we hoped that if we fiddled around long enough trying to find them, we would be told to forget it, especially if Saul and Del were mounting a diversion.

I know we were in Málaga for more than twenty-four hours and conspicuously parked near the port. I know that some of the interested parties possibly had prior warning, but it still surprises me to think how many people had managed to pick us up. Our departure from Málaga must have been quite a procession.

CHAPTER III

The road from Málaga to Granada must be one of the most beautiful roads in a country of beautiful roads, but it's not one to take in a bad temper, driving behind a man in a worse temper with whom you have to keep up, in a van you are not yet familiar with and which is bigger than anything you have ever driven before. For a start, the road gets up to one thousand metres in fifteen kilometres —an average slope of one in fifteen. Jo began by exclaiming at the tropical vegetation, then the view, and finally complaining of sickness. By the time we had got to Loja—just over half way—it was getting dark and we lost the benefit the easier road would have brought.

Fortunately there was no difficulty in Granada: we were on the Jaen-Madrid road almost before we were in the town. What with the mountains and the darkness it was about half past nine when we booked into the camp site.

It seemed a nice spot, as far as one could tell in the dark: under pines overlooking what appeared to be a small lake with mountains beyond. There was a restaurant too. However, Saul and Del were still very grumpy: indeed, would hardly talk to us. They weren't interested in food but cursed when they found the site shop was shut and they couldn't get any Coke for their rum. In the end Del talked the barman into selling her a large 'familia' sized bottle over the counter and that was the last we saw of them.

Jo and I had a pleasant meal in the restaurant—half a chicken each, roasted with garlic, chips and salad, and a bottle of Rioja *blanco*—had coffee and a *coñac*, and retired to our van. Fortunately Jo seemed to have forgotten her fantasies about labels. We sorted out the back seats, making a passable couch out of them, and were soon asleep, oblivious of the characteristic noises of the Spanish camp site: guitars twanging, an Aussie whistling *Waltzing Matilda*, and the toc-toc-toc of hammer on aluminium pegs as a late arrival put up his tent.

I awoke with Jo pulling at my shoulder. She was already dressed.

'If you get out and go to the toilets or whatever, I'll be able to make some coffee.'

I gathered together a towel and wash-bag and padded off through the pines. The sun was already well up and so were most of the campers. I had to queue at the wash-basins behind a robed, fat Frenchman, and a very bronzed, very large, very muscular Australian in the very briefest of shorts. He gave me a huge grin, flashing a set of immaculately white and even teeth.

'Been here long, sport?' he asked.

'Er, in Spain?'

'Where else, sport?'

'No actually. Landed at Málaga yesterday.'

'From Morocco? Get you! But you must have come down through Spain first to get there, yes?'

Well, of course Saul and Del had. Fortunately, at this moment the Frenchman moved off.

'Excuse I, sport. Time to get cleaned up for another day in sunny Spain.'

When my turn came at last I found that the water was cold and my razor blade blunt.

'Oh, you poor dear, you have scraped yourself,' said Jo, when I got back. Fool thing to say, but she had made a reasonable cup of coffee, and found her way to the shop and bought a packet of *madalenas*, sweet sponge cakes, which I rather like. I began to feel better.

'Others up yet?' I asked, looking across at the blue van, about ten yards away.

'Not a murmur.'

'Oh well, let them sleep in a bit longer. They had a rough day of it yesterday.'

'All right. But I would like to get on. I shan't be able to think of anything but that hash till we get back.'

I looked at her. Certainly she seemed hollow-eyed and tense.

'Right you are, old girl. It is a bit of a strain, I know. Two days and we'll be in France, and then if we really push it we'll make Dieppe the next night or early the following day, and it'll all be over.'

But she wasn't to be comforted that easily.

'You called Del a "great girl". I'd rather not be your "old girl".'

I sighed—not too obviously, I hope.

However, the surroundings, now we could see them, were too impressive to allow one to remain irritated for long. We were in a little pine wood on a small plateau about twenty feet above the lake, which was in fact a reservoir with a small dam about half a mile along the bank from where we were. In the other direction were the restaurant, offices and so on, and a more gentle slope down to the water to something like a beach. Here some children were splashing about stirring up the white clayey mud. All very decent, if rather obviously man-made. But then the lake spread out deep blue; far on the other side were grassland and farms; then olive groves, and finally

75

the six-thousand-foot peaks of the Sierra Herana. Altogether it was an enchanting spot.

I finished my *madalena*, poured another cup of coffee and lit a cigarette.

'It's a nice spot,' I said.

'I wish you'd go and wake them.'

'In a minute.'

'Now.'

'Oh, all right.'

Saul's van—well, it was as much mine as the one I drove: I had paid for both—was unconverted and had no windows behind the driver's door. I banged on the metal side. No answer. I banged again.

'Bugger off.'

I went back to Jo and reported. She shrugged—at my weakness I suppose—and pulled an angry face.

While I was finishing my cigarette I amused myself observing the national characteristics of our fellow campers. There were the French: Madame was already preparing vegetables or salad for lunch; Monsieur was scrupulously cleaning his large Citroën. Shortly he would wash the even larger trailer. The Germans had improvised a volley-ball net. The Americans and the Australians—committed to doing every camp site in Europe in six months—had long since struck their tents and gone. The English, well that would depend. There was a middle-aged couple, the man on his tubular camp-chair reading an old copy of the *Daily Express* while his wife knitted; and there were the two shaggy youths sprawled out on sleeping bags by their Mini. Strange. The Mini had a Spanish, MA for Málaga, number plate. Yet I was sure they were British—and somehow familiar too.

'Those two with the Mini,' I said to Jo. 'They are British aren't they?'

'You mean the big fair-haired fellow with a spotty face and the mean looking dark one with greasy long hair? Yes, they're British. I heard them talking in the car-park yesterday.'

'In the car-park?'

'Yes, by the bull ring in Málaga. Quite a coincidence them being here, I suppose. When are you going to wake those two up?'

'Their Mini has Spanish number plates.'

'Well I expect they hired it. You can you know. When are you going to wake them up?'

I went over and banged again.

'Time to get up,' I called.

Nothing.

Another bang, then a light mocking laugh like—forgive me, but it really was—like silver bells. Then Saul's voice, with a thick, satisfied tone about it.

'For Christ's sake, Mark, sod off.'

I stood back for a moment and thought about it. Part of me resented the fact that it was my van and they ought to have done what I asked. Another part was deeply envious of what was going on in there. Lastly I thought, why the hell not, why shouldn't they? But I didn't too much want to face Jo about it.

'I don't think they'll be up for a bit yet,' I called out. 'I think I'll wander over to the shop and see if they've got razor blades.'

'You do that,' she said angrily. 'You'd be better out of my way, if that's the best you can do.'

I sauntered off moodily, found the razor blades, and then went down to the little beach where the children were playing. There was no need for Jo to get huffy, I thought. After all, it was virtually her idea, bringing Saul and Del along. The thing was, we had decided on the

77

Volkswagen, a posh converted one, and making ourselves look as respectable as possible, and then the thought of crossing three frontiers with thirty kilos of hashish had been too much. Then Jo had remembered how on an assignment to America—for *Nova* I think it was—she had returned with a few ounces and had dreaded that she might be done at Heathrow. But there had been a group of long-haired louts, a minor pop group she supposed them to be, on the plane, and she had had the idea of tucking herself in behind them at Customs. It had worked: they had been stopped and she had been let through. So we had had the idea of using two vans; the first, a decoy, as scruffy as possible, the second as respectable as possible with the hashish.

Saul and Del had jumped at the idea when I suggested it to them—and why not? The whole point of the plan meant that there could be no possible risk for them and I offered a couple of hundred pounds on top of expenses as well. I gave Saul the money to buy his van: he had found it in the yard of a shady south London car-dealer and, with its wooden floor, its blank blue-black sides, its touches of rust, and its spurious 'M' registration, it had just the right look to make any Customs official sit up and take notice.

About all this I mused as I idly tossed stones into the lake. And so far, apart from Saul overdoing it at Málaga and his quite justifiable lewdness this morning, it was working out very well. I wondered if Jo had calmed down enough to agree, and I stood up. A figure moved on the bank twenty feet above me—the fair-headed, unhealthily spotty Englishman. I ignored him and made my way up to the vans.

To my surprise Saul was now up, standing outside our van, chatting to Jo. He was bare to the waist apart from his absurd hat and a towel round his neck. His trousers khaki jeans—were very tightly cut and there was a sort of

78

animal insolence in his stance that did nothing towards improving my attitude to him.

'Hi!' he said. 'I was just coming to look for you. Jo didn't know where you had got to.'

'Hullo. You're up then.'

'Yup.' He yawned deeply, stretched his arms, scratched his crotch, and giggled. 'Yup. Soon be time for lunch I should think.'

'Time to be getting off,' said Jo, icily, from the back of the van where she was drying up our coffee things.

'Well, yes,' said Saul. 'Del asked me to have a word with you about that.'

'Oh?'

'Yes. You see she doesn't want to leave Granada without seeing the Alhambra. She's never been further south than Madrid, and the Alhambra is apparently something one ought to see.'

'Oh, Christ,' said Jo.

'Well actually, I sympathise with you,' said Saul. 'I'd hate to be sleeping on a load of hash that could get you six years in a Spanish jail. But Del does feel rather strongly that she wants to see the Alhambra. In fact I don't think she'll move on until she has seen it.'

'Why the little...'

'Steady on, old girl,' I interrupted. 'Look. I don't see why we shouldn't go. It's just possible the police still have half an eye on us after yesterday—perhaps we ought to make a bit more of behaving like tourists. Anyway, I'd like to see it too. Where is Del?'

'In the showers.' Saul's hand irritatedly slapped a mosquito on his freckled shoulder. 'That's OK then, is it? We go to this Alhambra? I don't suppose it'll take more than an hour or so, and then we'll be on the road to Madrid.'

CHAPTER IV

I suppose that on a trip involving four people who don't know each other all that well and who are not joined by ties of any great strength, there is a tendency for the relationships to shift; with the added tensions that go with serious smuggling, the emotional weather is even more likely to be changeable. Yet it's not easy in these matters to decide just at what point any individual crosses a threshold, or decisively changes direction. In spite of a night of more or less drunken stupor followed by a warm, lazy morning in absolute physical proximity Saul and Del were distinctly edgy with each other. In spite of or because of? Certainly it became obvious that her insistence that he should ask me about the Alhambra had needled him. She was a long, long time in the shower and that also needled him, and of course it drove Jo berserk. By the time she came out, dressed in a short bathrobe with her hair wrapped up in a towelling turban, and looking like a modern Venus rising from the waves, the other two were so annoyed with her that it would have been churlish of me not to come to her rescue.

'Hi!' she called, almost tripping along over the pine needles. 'Isn't this just a great place? Aren't those mountains beautiful?'

'You've been ages.'

'Oh! Oh! OK. But the shower was hot, Saul.' She made

wide eyes on the word 'hot'. 'It's the first hot wash I've had for a week.'

I made room for her in the wide side-door of the van so she could sit down. She began towelling her hair and the creamy softness of her breasts moved in the opening fold of her bathrobe.

'We'll never get to the Alhambra now,' Saul went on.

'Oh come on. I shan't be long—hair dries in no time in this heat, and it'll only take me five minutes to dress.'

'Do you know what the time is?' Jo asked.

'Nope.'

'It's half past twelve.'

'Oh no-o-o-o,' a long wail. 'We don't get to the Alhambra then. You're right. Saul, why didn't you tell me? You're a real pig.'

'What do you mean?'

'It'll shut at half past one. Sure to. Ohhhh!'

I took a quick decision.

'Look,' I said. 'Since Tangiers, we have all had a pretty beastly time. Let's give ourselves a holiday today. We'll really take our time, have a nice long lunch in the restaurant, laze about a bit, and get to the Alhambra at half past four. We'll come back here for the night and make a really early start tomorrow. By tomorrow evening we'll be almost as far as if we left now. Certainly way beyond Madrid. Now let's all take it easy for a bit.'

'How you can even talk about taking things easy...' There was a whine in Jo's voice, and I determined to pay it no attention.

We got up to the Alhambra at about a quarter to five after a not too unpleasant afternoon. Once she could see that we were determined to stay Jo simmered down, drank a bit at lunch and cheered up.

We parked outside the Palace of Charles V, bought our tickets—big blue paper ones with perforated bits for each place visited—and started off, round the Alcazabar first, the fortified part. There was nothing very startling here except the views over Granada to the high sierras which were magnificent. Jo and Saul began to make faintly mocking remarks about the point of climbing a tower several storeys high to see a view from a vantage point not spectacularly better than the one from the battlements below.

Then we moved to the Alcázar and they were effectually silenced. There is a still perfection about that succession of halls and courtyards which cannot fail to move. I think they are the most beautiful interiors I have ever seen: they have a simplicity, for all the complexity and geometrical intricacy of the detail, which surpasses the vulgar grandeur of Christian palaces. The Courtyard of Myrtles and that of Lions, the Hall of Ambassadors and of Justice, each, whether large or small, has its own unique perfection of light and shadow, of simple geometric tiles or exquisitely fine lacy stonework, of the play of water or the stillness of it, that is simple enchantment. Perhaps I was tired, perhaps I was just a shade tipsy, certainly I was in a state of emotional disturbance—but mainly I think it was the sheer beauty of these places that actually moved me to tears at times.

I could have spent hours there, but as the afternoon wore on and southern Spain stirred out of its siesta, the halls became increasingly crowded. One has heard how foreign tourists ruin Spain—this may be so; but the Alhambra that afternoon was the resort not of foreigners particularly, but of coachloads of Spanish families—and I mean families—grannies in black dresses, grand-dads in black berets, dads in shirt sleeves, mums in flaring summer dresses, and children, children, more children, and babes in arms. And they all had one ambition in common: to have themselves photographed by one of the uncles as a family group against one or other or all of the more notable features of the palace.

'Honestly,' said Jo, 'they've not come to look at the place at all, they just want their pictures taken.'

'Bloody photographers,' said Saul.

At this, I looked round quickly for Del who, like all Americans, never stirred abroad without a camera, and who, I thought, would be hurt by these remarks. But she had disappeared.

'Hang on,' I said, 'we've lost Del. I'll go and look for her.' And before either of them could suggest that Saul should go rather than me, I moved off.

We were in the Patio de los Leones at the time and I had to go back through all the principal areas before I found her—not that that was any great hardship, and it was good to see the places again without Saul and Jo and in spite of the crowds.

The Sala de Embajadores is a square room pierced on three sides with windows that overlook the city. These windows are marvellously and intricately carved and have deep sills which are just long enough for two people to sit in them together. In one of these embrasures I could see Del, her hair lit by the levelling beams of the late afternoon sun, her smock and jeans dappled with the shadows from the lacy stonework. The same light played over the man she was sitting with and talking to. I could not bring myself to wait long enough to be sure, but the painful kick I felt in my solar plexus left me feeling certain that I was looking at the back of Mike Chichester.

I dodged back down the side of the Patio de los Arrayanes

and into the comparative darkness of its cloister. It took
me a minute or so to recover and during that time I had
to question what I had seen. The man had been in a white
shirt with pale grey trousers; I had the impression that
his jacket dangled behind his back from one hand. I had
seen only his back, but there was that very glossy, curly,
black hair, the tan, a characteristic tilt of the head. No, my
reason was now insisting that I had not seen enough to be
sure it was him, but nevertheless I remained where I was
for a good two minutes and would have stayed there far
longer had not Del appeared, alone, at the end of the
long, still pool, exquisitely framed by the slender pillars
and arches behind her.

'Hi!' she called, as she saw me. 'Where did you get to
then? I've been all over for you.'

I edged out towards her.'

'Del. Don't be alarmed, but come here quickly,' I called
as soon as I was near enough to make myself heard without shouting. Looking puzzled, but far from alarmed, she
skirted a family group, careful not to get between them
and their cameraman, and joined me. I moved back into
the cloister.

'That man you were talking with, where is he now?'

'I don't know. I guess he's out on the parking lot. He just
said he had to go, looked at his watch, and went.'

'When?'

'Just now. Just as I saw you. I said to him "Here's one
of my party", then you disappeared again and off he
went too in the other direction. Say, what is this?'

'It's just possible that he is the man we're meant to be
smuggling for—Mike Chichester.'

'Jeeeesus, no!'

'But I didn't see him properly. Describe him to me.'

She did, but there was nothing in what she said that

could not have fitted many men. But she did mention, without prompting from me, that he had a marked gap between his front teeth.

'What did he say? What did you tell him?'

'Oh my, I don't know. Hey, can't we sit down? Look, he's gone, I'm sure of that,' she added, sensing my caution. We sat down on the edge of the stone floor of the cloister. 'Now let me see. Hey, you know, he was kind of inquisitive, now I think about it. I was taking a shot through the stone work of the roofs beyond, and he came up and talked about the view and so on, and what sort of camera I had. Then we sat down where you saw us, and he asked me how long I'd been in Spain, was I with friends, where was I staying, where were we going next.'

'What did you say?'

'I told him.'

'What?'

Patiently she ticked off on her fingers. 'Two nights in Spain since Morocco—I didn't tell him that one night was in the Málaga brig; yes, I was with friends; at a camp site on the Madrid road; Madrid. That's all. Then you showed, and vanished, and he disappeared too. Hey, Mr Elmer, none of that can be bad, can it?'

'Please stop calling me "Mr Elmer".'

'Oh. Sure, Mark.'

I gave her a quick half-smile and then got down to trying to think it all out. If it was Chichester, and I had to assume that it was, then his presence at the Alhambra was not coincidence. Somehow or other he must have been on our track already; he probably knew about the second van; and he certainly knew the camp site we were based at. Indeed he was perhaps already on his way there, confident that he did not need to follow us to be sure of keeping in touch with us. Probably he had cottoned on to our method

85

of smuggling the hash through Customs. If he had, he would be content to let us smuggle it into France, and possibly over the Channel too, before he moved in on us. But he had a problem: he had to keep in touch with us without our being aware of him. Already that had proved too difficult.

So, what were we to do? Obviously we must lose him. I tried to visualise the map of southern Spain.

Saul sat down beside me and I sensed Jo behind.

'OK?' asked Saul. 'Time to go? Jo wants to be ready for an early start tomorrow to be sure of getting beyond Madrid.'

'Seville,' I said.

CHAPTER V

But everything went wrong. The plan I concocted was that we should return to the camp site and wait there until the morning. Then, very early, as soon after dawn as possible, we would drive back into Granada and, assuming that Chichester was following us, take different routes, driving around the town, before finally setting out down the Seville road at about nine o'clock. We were to meet up again at Láchar, a small village about ten kilometres out of town. One of the apparent merits of this plan was that for the first sixty kilometres the road to Seville was also the road to Málaga and would surely be the last road Chichester would expect us to take.

Back at the camp site we had nothing to do but wait for nightfall, still about an hour away, and nothing to do with that hour but watch the sun set and the mountains change from gold to rose to blackness above the lake, and count the stars as they came out. That, and drink the occasional *Cuba Libre*. It was the latter, I suppose, that led us to be a little careless about how loudly we spoke to each other and what we said—but, really, assuming that Chichester was waiting for us outside somewhere, and there was certainly no sign of him in the camp, there seemed no great need for care or secrecy. Certainly I do remember that Del and I had a more or less shouted conversation from van to van, something like this.

'How far is Seville?'

'About two hundred and sixty kilometres.'

'It'll still be daylight when we get there?'

'Oh yes.'

'Will we see the cathedral?'

And so on. That was the first thing to go wrong, though it seemed harmless enough at the time. The thing is— Chichester was not there to hear and I had no idea that there was anyone else around interested enough to be listening.

The next two things to go wrong seemed equally innocent. We moved off at about seven o'clock in the morning, but first we had to pull up at the camp offices to reclaim our passports and pay our fees. As I let myself out of the van I noticed a tall fair-haired character loaded up with rucksack, sleeping bag and the rest leaning against the barrier, and I recognised the Australian who had been in front of me in the morning queue for washbasins the day before.

'Hi!' he called. 'You heading for Seville?'

And without thinking I answered, 'Yes.'

When I came back out of the camp site office he was sitting in the back of the van behind Jo and with his feet propped up on one of the green suitcases. Jo was looking very stonefaced.

'Hi, Mr Elmer. Do you mind if I call you Mark?' He grinned broadly. 'Your very good lady (he said "lidy") told me your name (nime). Excuse I, but I've asked myself along as far as Seville, no further than that I promise you.'

What could I do? I could hardly plead we had changed our minds about where we were going; he was far too big to threaten with physical violence and calling the police was, of course, right out of the question. For a moment I thought of appealing to traditional good manners and asking him politely but firmly to get down. But another long look at him made it clear that this would not work. He was so smugly sure of himself, so big from his curly fair hair to his bulging furry thighs and his walking boots, his smile was so broad, he was such a ruddy hunk of totally extrovert good humour that I realised that he just wouldn't believe me if I asked him to get out.

I shrugged acquiescence and climbed in. Saul came to the window.

'Anything I can do?' he asked.

'No, no, not at all,' I said bravely.

A moment or two later the blue van pulled out on to the road and I followed.

Of course our Australian friend talked and talked.

'Let's get acquainted,' he began. 'My name is Simon but that's a Pommie sort of label (libel), so call me Sime...' and he went on and on, about where he'd been, where he was going, and how he'd taken this year off before finally settling into his father's construction business in Sydney. And then he told us how 'dinkum' the van was, exclaimed at the amount of luggage we had, and was that can spare petrol, yes it was, and so on.

Soon we would be in Granada and the plan was that I should take evasive action to throw Chichester off the scent; how on earth was I going to explain that sort of manoeuvre to Sime? I looked in the driving mirror—yes, the manoeuvre would be necessary: a Seat 1200, white, was keeping awkwardly to a distance of about two hundred yards behind us.

Then the third thing went wrong and the problem of Sime was mysteriously solved. Saul's van broke down.

I was following quite closely behind him when suddenly he slowed down without any warning at all. I nearly hit his rear bumper. Then he jerked along a bit and finally settled down to steady progress at about eight miles an hour. Black smoke pumped out of the exhaust. After three minutes of this and in response to blasts on my horn and flashed headlights, he pulled into the side and we all got out.

The Volkswagen van engine is at the back and one gets at it through a sort of tailgate low down near the ground. Soon all three of us—Sime naturally wanted to look too—had our heads in the confined space while Jo and Del giggled behind us. They said it was the sight of three male bottoms pushed up in the air that brought that on. It soon became obvious that none of us was a mechanic; that the engine would run but that beyond a certain low speed it would not accelerate; that none of us knew why this should be so.

'I would reckie,' said Sime, 'that your fuel is not getting to the engine like it's meant to.'

We all straightened.

'Yup,' said Saul, 'I should think that explains it.'

'What do we do?' I asked.

'Limp along to the nearest garage?'

A Spanish practice that seems to me to be very sensible is that at the entrance of every town is posted the addresses of the agents for the more common makes of car. Five minutes later we reached this sign on the city boundary and learnt the whereabouts of the V.W. specialists; the *Nagel Guide* street map told us the way. Not that we needed this, for just then there was the angry racket of motor-bikes behind us and two guardias cruised up alongside. First they signalled at Saul to get a move on, then they flagged him down instead.

Jo began to look panicky but managed to restrain herself. Sime, however, really did seem frightened at the sight of those slick green uniforms and polished belts and boots.

As we pulled in behind Saul he spoke.

'Excuse I, sport, no offence intended, it's just that it looks like you'll be some time getting your cobber's van fixed. So I'll take the oppo of this stop and get on down the road. Maybe I'll see you in Seville. Bye now. Mrs Elmer, it was a privilege making your acquaintance. So long.' And he was out before we had properly stopped, striding off down the nearest side-street.

If it was the guardias he was nervous about he needn't have bothered—both were entirely engrossed with Del's appearance and fluent Spanish. At length they saluted smartly and remounted their machines. Saul ran up to us.

'Del's been marvellous. We're going to get a police escort all the way to the garage. Hullo, you've lost your drongo.'

'"Drongo"?'

'Austr-i-lian for creep.'

While the van was being dealt with—the mechanics said that it would take an hour—I suggested that we should walk round the neighbourhood and see if we could spot Chichester. Now there was more traffic it was impossible to say if one of the many white Seats about the place was the one that I had thought earlier might be his.

'Not me,' said Jo firmly. 'I'm not risking running into him. I'd be terrified.'

'No point in my going,' said Saul. 'I'll wait here with Jo.'

Del hesitated for a moment and then elected to come with me.

'I can tell you if I see the man I saw yesterday in the Alhambra and you can tell me if it's Chichester,' she said.

When we were outside I took her arm.

'Are things all right between you and Saul?' I asked.

She pouted. 'Sure. We had a bit of a row last night. Nothing really to bother about though.'

91

'Are you sure?'

'Hell, yes. Stop being avuncular. Let's enjoy Granada.' Marlene voice again.

By now the town had woken up and there was a general air of pleasant busyness in the streets. It was still cool, and there was a lot of water about as people sluiced down their pavements and opened up their shops. We got off the modern boulevard we were on and into the marvellous side-streets of the town with its high old buildings in pale ochres and browns, hidden courtyards, wrought-iron balconies and trailing geraniums. Del unaffectedly admired everything; exclaiming at a tiny shop with ceiling dark and festooned with sausages, at the sudden glittering cascade of sardines as a porter from the market emptied his basket in another. She caught my hand every now and then and called me Mark.

We passed a small gift shop and suddenly she stopped, pointing in the window.

'Oh look, Mark. All those leather wine bottles,' and she grabbed my hand and pulled me in. 'You ought to have one, you know. You can use water in them and they keep it marvellously cool. It's the evaporation.'

I couldn't see the point of all this but there was a mischievous glint in her eye. I picked one off the rack and began to examine it. It had an awful red and black picture of the Alhambra stamped on it.

'No, they're too expensive. Come on, let's go,' and she spun me round out on to the pavement and face to face with Chichester.

It was a dreadful confrontation.

For a moment we looked at each other and I could feel the blood leaving my face. He looked pale too, but uncertain as well, though his normally bonhomous eyes were narrowed and his lips compressed in a mask of anger or hate. Then suddenly he grinned, though his eyes remained cold.

'Proper little prick you are, aren't you, Elmer.' The upper class twang in his voice had never been so pronounced: the headboy who has caught a junior doing something distasteful behind the squash courts. 'But we'll see, we'll see.'

I reached for Del.

'Let's get back to the garage,' I muttered, and without looking behind I walked off.

'It was him, wasn't it?' she gasped, trotting to keep up with me. 'That's the man who spoke to me yesterday. I wanted you to get a close look at him. He's been behind us since we left the others. My, but didn't he look just too fierce for words?' She looked back. 'He's still there, you know.'

Back at the garage the blockage in the fuel pipe had been cleared, and they were about ready to go. I told them about Chichester.

'Oh my God!' cried Jo. 'He'll kill us. I'm sure he will.'

'Don't be silly.'

'You know he can turn us over to the police just any moment he wants to, you know that, don't you,' she went on more angrily.

'Look Jo, calm down. He won't do that. I've no doubt he'd like to, he might even want to kill us. But what he really wants is the...' I looked nervously round the big, factory-like workshop. There were mechanics everywhere, and the man at reception had spoken a little English. '...the you know what. I'm pretty sure he's on his own and for the time being all he can do is just keep on our tails. We'll keep to our original plan—split up to confuse him, chase round the town a bit, and meet at Láchar.'

When we drove out of the garage Chichester was not

to be seen. Nevertheless I did everything I'd read about in books about this sort of thing—crashed the lights at amber, turned suddenly down side-streets, and even took a one-way road the wrong way—until Jo was nearly in hysterics again for fear of the police—and after half an hour I was sure that there was no white Seat following me. There wasn't either. When we got to Láchar Saul and Del were waiting at the entrance to the village. I pulled up behind the blue van.

'Didn't work, did it?' said Saul.

'Why not?'

'Get out and look.'

Up the road twenty yards or so in front of the blue van was a white Seat 1200.

'Is that him?' I asked.

'Yup. Del had a closer look.'

'How the hell did he get here?'

'He seemed to be waiting for us as we left Granada.'

Del had joined us now.

'Tell him, Saul.' There was a note of ice in her voice. Saul blushed and pulled his stupid hat down over his face like a little boy.

'I told them at the garage we were going to Seville. Well, the reception man asked, he was just being matey, there seemed no harm. Chichester must have asked after us.' He looked up. 'What do we do now?'

I could have pushed his face in.

'For Christ's sake, I don't know. Go on to Seville and try to lose him there,' I said.

I don't know why I didn't say 'go back to Granada and lose him', it just didn't occur to me. By then the idea of going to Seville was stuck firmly in all our minds.

CHAPTER VI

The procession continued on its way in unbroken order—
Saul, then me, then Chichester—for about three hours and
one hundred and fifty kilometres, at which point Saul took
a wrong turning into the hill town of Estepa. At least I
think that was the name of the town: I've only been able
to confirm its name by looking at a map and that's the
name that seems to be in the right place. Approaching
this town from Granada one has the plain of the River
Genil to the right and the foothills of the Sierra de Yeguas
on the left, on the side of one of which the town is pre-
cipitously placed. Where the main road begins to skirt the
foot of the town there is a slightly confusing road junction
since there is a third road on the right signposted to
Herrera and Puente Genil. Thinking that he was avoiding
this secondary road, Saul took the left-hand prong of what
was in fact a three-pronged fork.

Almost immediately we were climbing extremely steep,
very narrow streets which hairpinned back and forth
between low white houses. At any other time these would
have been interesting—they looked very poor, many had
unglazed windows barred with black wrought iron, but
they were immaculately kept. The whiteness reflected the
one o'clock sun with a brightness that hurt the eyes, and
there was not a scrap of trash or anything, not even a
melon skin, on the cobbled stones. But with all the twists

and turns and the narrowness, turning and going back was out of the question. The only route was onwards and upwards. Suddenly the houses stopped and we were faced with an even steeper, unsurfaced track, which, with one more hairpin bend, took us to the very top of the hill. There it spread itself out into a car-park at the foot of a small but imposingly sited citadel.

I drew up beside the blue van and Jo and I sat tight to see what Chichester would do. The white Seat circled the little car-park and came to rest at the entrance to it about thirty yards away. We could see him clearly now, white shirt setting off his tan, and large sunglasses which hid whatever expression his eyes held. His strong brown fingers showed impatience at least, if nothing worse, drumming on the steering wheel, but he made no move towards us.

'Sorry about that,' Saul said at my window.

'Not to worry, no harm done. It looks a nice spot. Let's get out and stretch our legs.'

'Do you think we ought to?' asked Jo. 'I mean what about . . . ?' and she gestured towards Chichester.

'I don't see what he can do. I doubt if he'll leave his car anyway. One of us could easily double back and let his tyres down.'

'All right then. But stay close to me.'

The view was certainly magnificent. Framed between cypresses the town dropped away beneath us with startling steepness, a sort of narrow semi-circle of tiled roofs pushed up against each other, broken only by a church quite near the top. Beyond, the land rolled away, gently undulating towards the distant river, hill after hill covered in geometric patterns of olive trees. To the right there were steeper hills, some with rocky outcrops, rising, like the one we were standing on, four or five hundred craggy

96

feet above the plain. Behind us rose the grey walls of a small medieval keep and we could hear voices of workmen and the squeak of a pulley. Just then the flowing plaintive chant of some Moorish or gypsy lament unrolled itself through the clarity of the sparkling air, as one of the workmen, high on the battlements, recalled the despair of unrequited love. Well, I suppose that's what he was singing about.

Del made her usual comment.

'Hey, isn't this just great!'

We rounded a corner of the keep and came upon a wheelbarrow suspended sickeningly above our heads from a sort of derrick on the topmost pinnacle. A notice, decorated with the yoke and arrows of the Falange, proclaimed that restoration was in the hands of some ministry or other. The Flamenco lament ceased as the wheelbarrow load of cement reached the top.

'It is great,' I said and I meant it.

We strolled on and found ourselves outside a largish church, built into the fortifications and set above a real precipice which dropped a hundred feet to what looked like a line of Roman columns.

'Hey, you know what?' Del had finished taking photographs and a thought had come to her. 'When Saul took this turning, do you know what I thought he was doing?'

'Touch of the Steve McQueens to throw off your Chichester man?' suggested Saul.

'Don't be silly. There's not much Steve McQueen about you. No. There was a hitch-hiker just beyond the turning on the main road, and it looked like your Australian, and I thought you were trying to avoid him. Though why you don't like him, I don't know. *He* is a bit like Steve McQueen.'

All of which left us not quite unprepared for the odd

incident which occurred as we strolled back to a point just in sight of the cars and the track from the town.

Red-faced, for all his splendid physique, and bent beneath rucksacks and the arrow of the noonday sun, a figure had cleared the town and was struggling towards us. He paused, straightened, saw us, and waved. It was, indeed the dreaded Sime.

'Oh no,' I said. 'He'll want a lift again.'

'Can't he go with Saul and Del this time?' asked Jo.

'Not really, we've got no seats behind or windows for him to look out of. Though I wouldn't mind. I think he's dishy,' said Del.

Sime was now out of sight behind the cypresses and taking the last bend. He reappeared and drew level with Chichester in his white Seat.

In less than ten seconds Chichester was gone. Just like that. The ignition fired, the car shot forward, he spun the wheel and off he went, back down the way we had come, into the town, out of sight. That was the last we saw of him for days.

'Good gracious,' I said.

'Hi there!' The familiar drawl floated towards us. 'I thought it was you going up the hill, and I said to myself if I can get up to the top before they go, they'll get me the rest of the way to Seville.' He swung his rucksack off his back and sat on it. 'And I made it.'

He beamed with pride and a sort of cherubic, healthy innocence.

Just outside Seville the blue van pulled up again and Del came trotting down the pavement.

'Saul says if we're stopping here tonight there's one camp site on the Córdoba road and another on the road to Cádiz. Have you any preference?'

'No, not if the facilities are about the same.'

'And another thing. Since, um,' she looked at Sime, obviously unsure of what she could safely say in front of him, 'since, well, you know, your friend in the white car doesn't seem to be around, and you've decided to stop here anyway, would you mind if we went into the town and looked at the cathedral?'

Jo looked annoyed, but I didn't consult her. 'Yes, of course. Ask Saul to lead the way.'

'It would be crook to miss the cathedral,' said Sime from the back. His voice took on the note of awe that ex-colonials reserve for the wonders of the Old World. 'It's the third largest in Christendom, and the Giralda, a Moorish tower just next to it, must rank as one of the most striking relics of the Moorish occupation. It has no steps, but inclined planes, so the Arabs could ride two horses side by side up or down it.'

'Really?' I said.

But we never made it to the Giralda.

We cruised round Seville for some time before finding a parking place between the cathedral and the river and by then we were so hot and tired that the first thing we had to do was have a drink. Sime would not be shaken off—he wanted to see the cathedral, and he asked if we would take him on to the camp site afterwards. We found a café —too near the cathedral, so it was expensive—and I ordered beer for Saul and Sime, iced tea with lemon for the girls and a *café solo* for me. Del annoyed me by giggling at my pronunciation, particularly of *cerveza*—beer. Although it was not quite four o'clock there was plenty of traffic: the pavement was not wide and the petrol fumes were noisome. Sime and Del started to compare notes about Europe and especially Britain and this soon became a vehicle for teasing me. I could see now some of Sime's attractions—in spite of his appalling accent and manner of speaking he was not unintelligent and, with his Greek god-like good looks, athlete's physique and unfailing cheerfulness, I began to fear that he would make a real impression on Del. I think Saul began to share my fear. He entered into the repartee with some juvenile crack about gum trees and was smartly and cleverly put down. Del chortled.

I felt it was time to put an end to all this and called for the bill. A hundred pesetas. Absurd.

The three enormous doors in the west end of the cathedral faced the café, but all were closed. We began a long, long walk down the southern side which seemed to go on for ever. The architecture was dull—the stones blackened. The building, for all its size, seemed heavy and squat like an uninspired Victorian railway station. But this long straight pavement—almost deserted at that time of day with no shops or doorways—made it almost inevitable that one of us would at last realise that Chichester had not been our only tail.

Near the corner Saul paused and lit a cigarette.

'Stupid,' I said. 'You'll have to put it out in a minute.'

'Sod that,' he replied. Then, 'Hey. Look back there.'

'Look back where?' About a hundred yards behind us two faintly familiar figures paused and turned half away from us.

'Weren't those two staying at the Granada camp site?'

'Two English guys, you mean?' asked Del. 'One dark and greasy, the other spotty and blond. Yes, they were.'

Jo bit her lip. Like me she was remembering that they had also been in the Málaga car-park near the bull ring.

'Once you get on the tourist circuit you keep bumping into the same faces,' said Sime with irritating knowingness. 'Look how you keep bumping into me.'

We rounded the corner on to the east end of the cathedral and found the small door which the public are allowed to use to enter this, the third largest church in the world. We also found why all the other doors were shut: we were going to have to pay twenty-five pesetas each to get in and we were not going to be allowed in until half past four—another ten minutes. But at least we were now in shade. Low stone pillars supported a heavy chain which separated the small forecourt from the pavement and I sat down on one of these. Opposite me was a fountain—not playing—and beyond some rather interesting looking houses painted brightly in white, blue, green and red. Del came and sat on the chain, swinging herself to and fro.

'I think that over there must be the Barrio de Santa Cruz,' she said. As usual in touristical situations her thumb was in her guide book and her camera was unbuttoned. 'It used to be the ghetto and now it's meant to be an area of great beauty and atmosphere.'

I thought of persecution, burnings, the *auto da fé*.

The two men who had been following us came round the corner. The fair-haired one sat on the pillar next to mine and lit a cigarette—he was close enough for me to see that his thick mechanic's hands had dirty nails. The thin dark one leant over and whispered in his ear and sniggered. The blond gave the chain a yank that nearly put Del on the floor.

'Hey, watch what you're doing,' she cried.

But my skin had gone icy cold and I was nearly sick with fright. The fair-haired one, grinning now like his sly greasy mate, was massaging a heavy ring on his right hand —a skull with red stones in the eye-sockets.

'Mr Elmer, isn't it?' he called across to me and his voice brought back with shattering clarity the feel of the garage floor behind my flat in Ventleigh, the agony and the bitter taste of bile. He glanced up at his companion beside him. 'Mr Elmer's still mixing with very shoddy company, isn't he, Paco?'

'Very shoddy, Charley.' The dark one, Paco, had a slight accent. I realised he might be Spanish, or half-Arab, half-Spanish.

'Company he doesn't really know about, eh Paco?'

They sniggered again, then Charley got up, came over, and stood above me. Del edged away.

' 'Cos there's one sort of company Mr Elmer doesn't want to mix with one little bit, not with what he has in his van, eh Paco? What you'd call your guardia civils, in your lingo, right Paco? Remember that, Mr Elmer.'

Insolently he flicked his butt-end over my shoulder and Del had to move to avoid it.

As from a distance I heard Jo calling, saying that the cathedral was now open.

Darkness and size are the two most impressive character-istics of Seville cathedral. The increasing crowd that had gathered outside was swallowed and dispersed in that giant black maw. Del and I followed one group for a time into what appeared to be some sort of treasury in the south-east corner; I have never seen so much silver and silver gilt in my life, but most of it tasteless, religiose, and not always clean. We moved through three or more rooms in the same area and slowly my distaste for the ugliness of so much pointless wealth—even the paintings, some really good, were tattily framed and hung—overcame and pushed out of the front of my mind the shock of fear that had punished me outside.

'Do you like any of this?' I muttered.

'Not a bit,' and she took my hand and squeezed it. 'Let's get back into the main part.'

We walked down the most southern of the five naves past a succession of baroque chapels where bleeding tormented Christs writhed on their crosses and saints suffered even more exquisite martyrdoms, and everywhere there was the dull, heavy sheen of massive silverware beneath the soaring thickness of black, gothic pillars.

'Where have the others got to?' I asked.

'I don't know. Isn't that Sime over there?'

She indicated the far end of the nave, where a narrow strip of white-hot light lay in a long thin line beneath the closed gateway. Dimly I could see the tall Australian, his golden head thrown back to search out some detail high above him.

'Hey, those two awful men are there too,' Del cried.

Again the bitterness of fear in my mouth.

The three figures came together and then, very quickly —a dull thud, a stifled cry, a hoarse animal grunt. The group separated: two figures flitted silently along the west wall and disappeared into the gloom. The third, already on his knees, swayed and then, pushed forwards by the weight of his rucksack, slumped over.

Del reached him first. There was blood on his face and all over his shirt. In that dark place, filled with so much spurious suffering, Sime looked like yet another martyred saint. In agony more picturesque than his St Lawrence twisted on his red hot grill above him.

CHAPTER VII

Sime had not lost consciousness, though he was very pale. He wriggled and then grimaced.

'Can't move. Get me out of this bastard rucksack.'

Del and I struggled with the straps—even in that awful situation my throat tightened when our fingers met and when my elbow brushed the softness of her breast—and I got blood on my shirt. At last he was free and able to sit up.

'Cripes, I thought they'd done for me that time. But I don't think they have.' He was feeling round the knife wound in his side. Suddenly he chuckled. 'Like a stage stabbing: between arm and chest. The buckle on my rucksack must have deflected it.'

There were five or six more people round now and hurrying footsteps brought others nearer. Questions, answers in whispered Spanish, and the words *policía* and *médico* repeated. Jo arrived.

'What happened?'

'Those two who were following us. They stabbed Sime.'

She gave a whimpering, shuddering cry.

'It's all right. He's bleeding a bit, but it's only a flesh wound.'

'They'll get the police, we'll all be questioned. Oh Mark, what are we to do? We can't stay here with him.'

There was a surprised gasp from the crowd. Sime was on

his feet, keeping himself steady with an arm on Del's shoulder. Upright he looked an even more nightmarish figure than before: blood was smudged over almost all his shirt and on his shorts. His face was deadly pale.

'Mr Elmer, old son,' he said. 'I don't want to be an embarrassment to you and your lady (lidy) wife. No need to hang around. I shan't say you gave me a lift here. The fuzz are coming. You'd better be off. Bye now.'

A priest arrived while he was speaking and a purposeful clatter of heavy heels marked the approach of two municipal policemen. Del slipped from under his arm.

'Mr Elmer. I'll see you around. Look after yourselves.'

We hurried away past the winking candles and beneath the sightless eyes of marble saints.

After a muttered consultation at the road-side where the vans were parked we drove to the camp site on the Córdoba road. I let Saul find the way and so I had time to think a bit before we got there and by the time we arrived I had decided what must be done.

The site was quite a pleasant one—it had a swimming pool—but crowded and we found ourselves on the periphery with no shade. It was also near the airport and planes kept thundering over. Since it was only just gone five o'clock it was still very, very hot. I called Saul and Del over and we tried to make ourselves comfortable in my van, but it wasn't easy, not even with all the doors and windows open and the curtains drawn, and with glasses of tepid lemon squash.

'Right,' I started, 'it's quite obvious that this whole business has become a very nasty business indeed...'

'Look, before you go any further,' said Saul, 'will you tell us just what you think is going on?'

I wiped my brow and sighed a little. Really, Saul could be irritatingly obtuse at times.

'I should have thought it was all obvious enough,' Jo began. 'Sime had some petty quarrel with those roughs—probably something which blew up in a camp site, over a girl perhaps.'

'Hey, just a minute,' Del chipped in. 'They spoke to you outside Mark, didn't they? They knew you.'

'Look,' I said, 'please, all of you, be quiet, and let me get on.'

'There's no need to shout,' from Jo.

'I wasn't shouting...' Fortunately, at this point a jet bombed by overhead and gave us twenty seconds or so for reflection.

'We're listening, Mark,' said Saul, when it had gone.

I drank some lemon.

'Right,' I repeated. 'First, you ought to know that the two men who attacked Sime were the two who attacked me last April in Ventleigh.'

This took a moment or two to sink in, although all three of them had heard the story. Jo cottoned on first.

'You mean,' she said, and the note of fear, a sort of anxious whine that was becoming familiar, was more noticeable than ever in her voice, 'you mean that the people who said you were never to go near Chichester—they said they were from a Mr Jones didn't they?—have somehow found out where we are. And what we're doing, too.'

'Well, obviously. It's not a coincidence that they are here or that they were in Málaga and Granada.'

'But they don't seem to be following us. I mean not in the way Chichester was this morning. They just seem to turn up where we are. How do they manage to do that?'

'Look. Please let me say what I've worked out. Then you

can tell me where I may be wrong. OK?'

'Oh, all right.'

'Right then. Those two—Charley and Paco,' the ridiculous names thickened my voice with disgust, 'attacked me at Ventleigh, and said that a Mr Jones wanted me to have nothing to do with Chichester. We reckoned then that they belonged to some rival of Chichester. Well, it seems reasonable to suppose that that is still true.'

'In other words,' Saul interrupted again, 'we've got two gangs of thugs after us now, instead of one. Well done. I had about worked that out already.'

'Oh Saul, do let him finish,' said Del. 'How does Sime fit in? Why did they attack him?'

'I'm not sure about that. But did you notice how in that village with the castle when Sime arrived Chichester pushed off? And we haven't seen him since? Right, I think Sime was working with or for Chichester, and once he had met up with us again, Chichester could push off. And that's why those two thugs knifed him—he was one of Chichester's lot and had to be discouraged or removed. Outside the cathedral they said we were mixing with some odd company.'

'Oh, I don't go along with that,' said Del.

'Why not?'

'I liked Sime. I don't think he's a crook.'

'Is that all? You just like him, nothing else?'

She thought for a moment.

'No, I guess not. I just like him, so he's not a crook. Go on.'

'Right. Now the point I'm trying to make is this. We got you and Saul into all this because there didn't seem to be any way in which you could come to any sort of harm. I mean you weren't doing any smuggling, nobody need even have connected you with us in any way other than people casually travelling together. But now there is danger for you. We saw what happened to Sime. You know what happened to me. I think it's more than likely that Paco meant to kill him. It was nasty. I mean *really* nasty.'

We sat for a moment in the heat and remembered Sime's white face and the blood on his shirt.

'It was like something out of ... oh, I don't know—*Richard the Third*,' said Saul.

'For Christ's sake be serious,' cried Del. 'He was hurt and bleeding. All right, Mark, what do you want us to do?'

'I want us to separate. Split up. We can fix a time and a frontier post between France and Spain and reach it by different routes. We're the ones they are after, we have the hashish and that's what they want. You keep away from us except to do our frontier routine and you should be safe. There. That's what I wanted to say.'

'There was a silence. Saul lit a cigarette—one of those really foul cheap Spanish ones. I could see Del didn't like it either. Jo, I suppose, was immune through smoking Gauloises all the time.

'I'm not too sure I like it,' he said. He studied his nails and nibbled at one. 'Apart from anything else, there's the van. It could break down again anywhere. You've no idea what a wreck it is. No, I'm not joking. I really don't fancy being on my own somewhere if it goes again.'

'You've got Del. She speaks Spanish.'

Del moved restlessly. 'I don't like it either. I want to stay near you.'

'But why?'

She shrugged. 'Oh, I don't know.'

But the smile she gave me was melting from under lowered lids.

'Well, OK,' I said at last. 'We'll stay here tonight. Think

it over. I think you'd be better away. Indeed, I think I have a responsibility to see you do keep away.'

'Good on you,' said Saul. 'Come on Del. We'll talk it over and tell you at supper time. Shall we have a cook-up or go to the restaurant?'

'Restaurant,' said Del, firmly.

When they were gone I looked at Jo.

'You didn't have much to say.'

'No.' She pursed up her lips and gave a neurotic little wriggle. 'No.'

'Why not?'

'I said my bit and you paid no attention.'

'What do you mean?'

'I asked you how your two thugs always knew where to find us without following us.'

'Well, how the hell do I know?'

'Hasn't it occurred to you,' her voice rose and she began to push each word home with a little prod at the seat, 'that one or both of your precious young friends you think so much of, could be telling them, could be Mr Jones's spy?'

'Oh, what a ridiculous, stupid thing to say.' I felt really angry.

She shrugged her shoulders, pettishly.

'You see. They'll have a darned good reason for not splitting up. You see.'

Jo was turning out to be more of a burden than I had expected—it seemed to me that her chronic state of anxiety had taken a turn for the worse. She struck me now as suffering from paranoia: I tried to argue with her reasonably about her suspicions and she just would not listen; refusal to listen to reason is a classic symptom of paranoia. I soon gave up—she began to be tearful again.

I felt hot, sticky, frustrated, frightened. I gathered up towels, a change of clothes, soap, and so on, and went off to the showers; but that didn't bring much relief—in the little cubicle, with no clothes on and the almost cold water hissing round me, I felt peculiarly defenceless. I remembered Sime so well—his pallor, the blood, the thick darkness of the cathedral. Perhaps I also had in mind unconscious recollections of *Psycho*—at any rate I suddenly felt I could see my own blood swirling down the shower plughole. I turned the water off and began to dry myself. Voices, doors banging, the hollow echoing of such places. Two people coming in, two men, they could be Charley and Paco. If a jet went over not even shouts for help would save me. I blundered out of the cubicle and swung round into the washbasin area in such a hurry that I tripped and fell quite heavily against one of them.

They were German—young, short-haired. The one I had bumped into steadied me and said something I couldn't follow.

'Sorry, I'm English. So sorry. Please excuse me.'

'I say, old fellow, are you quite sure you are all right?' The accent was almost perfect—only the vowels were very careful.

'Yes, yes, thanks. Quite all right. I just tripped, that's all.'

He shrugged with easy insolence and turned back to his companion. I stumbled out into the sunlight. I looked around. Everything seemed perfectly sane and ordinary: some children were washing up in the big stone sinks; three bikini clad girls came from the direction of the swimming pool; two young Englishmen, excruciatingly dull in appearance with glasses, moppy hair, insecure grey flannel trousers, and sandals with socks, were putting up a tiny blue tent next to their brown Morris Minor. I really must take a grip on myself, I thought. My fears in the showers had been groundless, hallucinatory. It was absurd to have such a sense of hidden menace on a perfectly ordinary, slightly scruffy camp site. Yet, I don't know: there was the van and in it thirty-six thousand pounds' worth of hashish, and, however outrageous it seemed now there was no escaping it—Sime had been stabbed, just as surely as I had been beaten up at Ventleigh.

'Well, I hope your shower has improved your temper,' Jo said, as I returned.

'Yes. I suppose it has. But I could do with a drink.'

'Look, it's only half past six now. There won't be any food in the restaurant until half past nine at the earliest ...'

'So?' I asked.

'Well, if you're going to start in on the rum and Cokes now, you're going to be stoned out of your mind by nine o'clock.'

'Oh really!'

I finished dressing in silence.

'I'm going to the bar for a beer,' I said when I was ready. 'OK?'

'I take it I'm not asked.'

'No, you're bloody not. Not, at any rate, until you can talk to me with a little civility.'

The bar-restaurant-pool complex was a pleasant area laid out round an octagonal courtyard with a small fountain in it. I had just decided on a table when Del appeared from the pool; she came and sat beside me.

'You look marvellous,' I said.

'I must look a fright.' Her hair, and much of her young, supple, nut-brown body were wet. Her bikini was very small. She rubbed her hair and grinned across the table at me.

'What would you like?' I asked.

'What do you think I would like from you?' she said. I could not detect any mockery in her tone.

'I mean to drink.' I was blushing now.

'*Cuba Libre*, please.'

A waiter was hovering.

'*Un Cuba Libre con ron y una cerveza, por favor,*' I said, very carefully, pronouncing the word for beer as correctly as I could—'thairbetha'.

'Oh, well done, Mr Elmer,' she covered her mouth in mock horror. 'Oh, I am sorry. It just slipped out. Mark. But that was really good.'

The waiter didn't think so. He was a cheeky looking young sod and everything about Del, and especially the way her cold nipples showed through her bikini, had registered on him.

'*Un Cuba Libre y una "sairbessa",*' he repeated, correcting my pronunciation.

'Christ, what did he do that for? I thought you said I had it right.'

'Oh, sweet, you did,' and her still moist hand covered mine. 'But he's an Andalusian, and they say "s" for "th". And he's making a thing of it, maintaining his regional identity and all that.' Suddenly she pulled back her hand. 'Where's Jo?' she asked.

'Sulking,' I said. 'She wouldn't come.'

'Are you having a row?'

'Not really. We're not close enough for the term to have that sort of meaning. We only met through this business, you know.'

'Yes, I know. It's a bit like that with Saul and me. I was never taught by him, you know. I got on all right with him to begin with, but I'm getting a bit fed up with him now. Now you, of course, you're different.'

'Oh come on.'

'Yes, you are. For two years I had a hell of a crush on you.'

Her hand came back to mine and suddenly we were looking intently at each other. The moist tip of her tongue ran round her top lip and vanished.

'Look, I must be twenty years older than you.'

'Oh sheeee-it,' she said. 'What has that got to do with it? You're hellish good-looking, you're clever, and you're fun to be with. Here are our drinks. Mark. Get Saul out of that van tonight. It's quite warm enough for him to sleep outside in his sleeping-bag. Or perhaps Jo will have him.'

I took a long swallow of icy beer. I could hardly credit what she was suggesting.

Dinner, when we had it, was an awkward meal. Del kept making up to me, Jo was still moody, Saul unusually silent. I wondered what had occurred between him and Del during the couple of hours between the drink we'd had and the beginning of the meal. We still had a point to settle before the sleeping accommodation was rearranged. I returned to it when we had all been served a delicious fry-up of mixed sea-food.

'Have you talked over my suggestion about splitting up?' I asked.

'Oh yes,' said Saul. 'And it's just not on. Nice of you to mention it though.'

'Why not?'

'Well, there's the van bit I've gone into already. But also I don't see that we would be any less at risk away from you than with you. I mean they know how we work the frontier bit and that that is the connection between us. They know that you're carrying the hash. So, the only reason Del and I could be in danger would be if they threatened us as a means of blackmailing you. You know —kidnapped Del as a way of getting you to give up the hash. That sort of thing. And they'd be more able to do that if we separate than if we stay together. So there's no point in our separating.'

'OK, thanks. Well now, what's our next move? There's no point in staying here, though we're probably safe enough. I've been looking at the map. I suggest we take a route up through Mérida, Cáceres, Salamanca, Valladolid and Burgos. It's about as direct as one could wish. When we get to Burgos we can decide on what to do, depending on what we've seen of the opposition in the meantime.'

'Right. Burgos it is. Can we get there in one day?'

'Probably. If we make a really early start and keep going all the time. But we'll get as near as we can.'

There was an awkward silence while we chewed on squid and mussels. I felt Del squeezing my thigh. Jo suddenly stood up. Saul just managed to catch her glass before it spilt.

'I've had enough of this,' she cried. She turned on Del. 'Don't think I don't know what your game is, my girl. I'm on to you. I know why you won't go off on your own with Saul,' and she turned on her heel and marched out.

'Oh, Christ,' said Saul. 'I suppose something like this was bound to happen.'

'Don't you think you'd better go after her,' said Del, looking at me.

'Oh! Do you think I should? All right then. But wait for me here.' I left them. They looked worried and concerned.

Jo must have run. She was almost at the van before I caught up with her.

'Look,' I began. 'Listen, Jo. I don't see why you should be like this. It was clear from the start that there was to be nothing between us, that emotionally you still belonged to your husband, and that you wanted him back...'

'Stop it, stop it, stop it,' she was almost screaming now. I looked round to see how the other campers were reacting. 'Mark, you really are the most conceited little prick if you think I'm the least bit jealous. I don't care if you fuck every teenager between here and Dover. But can't you see what she is doing? Can't you see how her little game would have been ruined if you sent her away? She's got you and Saul really sewn up, hasn't she? God, men are stupid!'

'Oh Christ, woman,' I was really angry now. 'You don't still think she's spying on us, do you?'

'Of course she is, you fool.'

'You're mad. You really must be mad. It's the only word for it.'

'Look,' she said. 'Someone tells these people where we are. It's not me. It's not you. Saul, for all his faults, is honest and a good friend of yours. So it has to be that little bitch.' Then, very slowly. 'The first time you saw Chichester she was talking to him. Right?'

I wanted to hit her, but I managed to stop myself.

'All right, then,' I said, with heavy sarcasm. 'She's a spy. That's what you've got against her. And so I take it you don't mind if I go to bed with her?'

Jo was quiet. When she spoke it was with a sort of cold finality.

'Mark. All I want is to get back home with my share of the loot. When I have, I shan't want to see you again, or hear of you, or even remember I ever knew you. Sleep where you like. But get this. I'm not leaving the van or the hash, nor will I have Saul in here with me. Right? Good. Good night.'

CHAPTER VIII

It had been a very long, very tiring day and I felt absolutely drained of energy when I went back to the restaurant. After all it was still less than thirty hours since I had seen Chichester in the Alhambra—and an awful lot had happened since then. It must have shown in the way I approached the table.

'Oh my, look at him,' cried Del. 'You look shagged. Quick Saul, order him another *Cuba Libre*.'

'I'd rather have a coffee and a *coñac*.'

Saul made the order. 'How's Jo?' he asked.

'She's OK. I'm sorry about that. I think she'll go to bed now.' I stumbled on, realising that Saul himself was the problem now. 'She's got sleeping pills. She'll be all right.' I ended lamely.

'Yes,' he said. Then he looked at me, his tinted specs catching the light. He grinned. 'I think I'll buy a bottle of *coñac* and take a wander round the site. Never know what I might pick up. Del, I know you don't like having me too close when I've had a few, so why don't you leave my sleeping bag outside the van?' He stood up. 'Have a good night, my dears,' and he faded away towards the bar.

'Do you believe ladies should have orgasms?' Del asked.

'Oh, God!' I gasped. 'Yes. Of course I do.'

'Good.' She sounded almost brisk. Suddenly I wanted not to be so bloody tired.

Actually I need not have worried. I think the way the blue van was arranged had something to do with it. I have said how it was a completely unconverted delivery van with no windows and no fittings. Saul and Del had piled their very few belongings up on the raised area at the back above the engine leaving a space almost exactly five feet square between the engine and the driving seats. This was covered with cushions and pillows. A curtain on a piece of string could be pulled across between this area and the windscreen. It was lit by a dull interior light. Thus we were in a very comfortable, completely enclosed sort of cave which was just big enough to allow easy movement, but not large enough to allow any distraction to take our minds off each other's bodies.

In those hot days Del wore only three garments and they were soon off. Naked, with her long, long chestnut hair falling about her shoulders, over her breasts, or tossed to cascade down her back she made that warm cave into a treasure house far beyond any fantasy I had ever allowed myself to indulge in. For a long time we just played— moving slowly, tenderly, silently around and over each other, smiling and occasionally laughing quietly. Tension ebbed away from my body; exhaustion and the nightmare of Seville from my tired mind. The soft suppleness of her brown body, the delicious curves of firm breasts and buttocks created another, more delightful tension and our movements became quicker.

When we had come we lay diagonally across the space, I with my knees slightly raised and she with her head pillowed on my shoulder.

'When, you know, it happened,' she murmured, 'you

looked like a sixteen-year-old with his first girl.' I squirmed pleasurably, but she went on, more disconcertingly—'Most men do.'

I awoke a little before dawn and went to the toilet. The fears of sudden attack that had plagued me the afternoon before now seemed very absurd. It was cool and dewy. Saul lay between the vans with his hat set over his eyes, but I must have woken him with the noisy side door of the van. He tipped the brim of his hat and winked when I came back.

Del was awake too, of course. We made love again and then I fell into that really deep, warm, early morning sleep that seems the most perfect balm one can imagine, the sleep which never lasts long enough and which is very difficult to wake from.

Saul was banging on the tinny side of the van. Each bang was like a nail driven into my head.

'Go away.'

He laughed, and I had to too—remembering that this was what had happened at Granada two mornings before.

'It's half past nine,' he called. 'You were going to make an early start. For Burgos, remember?'

Del rolled over, yawning and stretching. Her hand found its way to my crotch and moved gently.

'Tell him to go away,' she murmured.

'I already have.'

'Oh go on. Tell him.'

'Saul,' I called. 'Just half an hour. Please.'

'Oh,' Del flounced away in disgust. 'Only half an hour!' Then she came back again.

'Mark. It's nearly eleven o'clock. And look. Jo says she'll drive your van off, and the you-know-what, if you don't get up quick. She says I can go with her and have your half share.'

We were on the road by a quarter to twelve, in our usual order—Saul and Del in the front in the blue van, Jo and I behind.

Jo maintained a surprisingly good temper throughout most of the day, and this made me want to please her. It was not that I felt guilty at the way I had treated her, but simply that I had expected her to be unpleasant at best and downright bad-tempered at worst, and when I found she was neither I felt grateful. Things went well in other ways too, at least to begin with. In the first place there was no sign of any followers behind us. After an hour or so I felt quite sure of this. In the second place I saw a hoopoe, and that was thanks to Jo too.

We were in a fairly lightly forested area perhaps a hundred miles north of Seville, with mountains near but not actually on top of us, when suddenly Jo cried out.

'Look, Mark, that bird. Didn't you see it?'

'No, tell me.'

'On a bush. It was quite big, and all black and white striped and just as we drew level it raised up a beautiful fan of a crest. Look there's another.'

I sounded the horn, flashed the lights, and slewed into the side. Of course, the noise I made frightened the hoopoe off into the woods, but I knew he was there and in what direction. The blue van had disappeared round the next bend, but I wasn't bothered. Either they had heard me and would turn back at the next opportunity, or, with the newer, better engine I would soon catch them up. I gathered up my binoculars, locked up the van and, with Jo behind, set off into the wood which was a mixture of ilex and deciduous oak. The ground was a dry, aromatic patchwork of lavender and sage. We had not gone far before we saw the flash of wings and heard the deep 'hoo-poo-poo' which gives the bird its name.

Stalking rather more carefully now we came up on them, two pairs, on a rather more open grassy piece of ground. We were actually within fifty yards of them. They were very handsome with their honey-coloured heads and necks, their long curved beaks, and then the startling contrast of pitch black and fierce white stripes in the tail and wings. But their most beautiful feature, which Jo had spotted, was their fan-like crest. Feeling very satisfied we walked back to the road.

'Was it nice last night?' Jo asked, quite quietly.

Suddenly I realised how good she was trying to be.

'Yes. Very.'

'Well that's fine. It really doesn't matter to me. But Mark, watch out for her. No, please don't be angry. Just keep an eye on her, and let's keep going. No more stops at places of "interest" where she can wander off on her own. OK?'

'OK.'

I squeezed her hand gratefully.

The blue van appeared on the other side of the road just as we got back. They had not been able to turn safely for some two miles what with the bends and the narrowness of the road and all the time they had been worried thinking that we had had a breakdown. They were quite peeved to learn that we had been hoopoe spotting.

We drove on for another hour or so and reached Mérida just before half past three. Saul pulled up at a filling station on the outskirts of the town and while we were filling up Del came over to us. The sight of her again filled me with a real surge of delight—she looked jolly and she gave me a secret smile, full of promise.

'Hey, do you know about this place?' she asked.

'Not really.'

'*Nagel* says it has the best preserved Roman theatre in Spain. Rebuilt by Hadrian. Say, that must have been Hadrian of the Wall, yeah? We can spare an hour or so, can't we?'

Jo nudged me gently. I wished that she hadn't, it wasn't necessary; I would have refused anyway.

'No, Del, sorry. If we keep going like this we'll make Burgos by midnight—if we mess about now, in the middle of the afternoon, get hot and so on, we won't feel like moving again and I doubt if we'll get even as far as Cáceres.'

'Midnight! You want to drive to midnight? Oh pooooeeee! Sheee-it! Oh well. But I warn you,' and her voice took on a touch of menace, albeit girlish, 'I shall be so bored and tired by then that I shall go straight to sleep.' She turned away and her hair flung out and floated down over her back. Then she turned again. 'OK. But you stopped for your hoopoes. No Roman theatres, no more birds. Right?'

So we drove through Mérida. Silly really as I understand the ruins are remarkable.

The landscape now became progressively more arid, the views to distant mountains more spacious, the villages less frequent and poorer. Jo wanted to comment on Del's attempt to get an extended stop but I wouldn't listen to her absurdities and she soon had the sense to shut up. We bypassed Cáceres with its Roman and Moorish walls rising above and still visible amongst the sprawl of industrial constructions that surround it. The map seemed to promise relief with a group of lakes round the Tagus, but these proved as bleak if not bleaker than the rest of the landscape being the very new, very neat shores of reservoirs achieved by damming the river many miles downstream.

The sun began to sink and its beams touched the twelfth-century walls of Plasencia with gold and rose, but we thundered on.

Our surroundings improved as we climbed up into mountains again towards Béjar, but the bends became really troublesome, especially just beyond the very pretty township of Baños de Montemayor, where we were often swung full-face into the sun. Once over the pass and through Béjar the road settled down again and after almost eight hours' driving it became a little difficult not to dream. Dream, what of? Pleasant things mostly. Of Del. Of Jill. Not bad in less than six months for a man nearing forty. Of hoopoes. Shame really not to be paying more attention to the birds. Many species in Spain rare elsewhere. One or two not to be found anywhere else at all. Wonder how Del will be tonight. Good of Saul: hope the sleeping-bag is not too uncomfortable. And the steady roar of the soporific engines as we bundled along in slowly gathering twilight, through ilex forests again. Strange landscape, so like an artificial park with the trees standing neatly equidistant from each other, the foliage black and glossy, and each one shaped by sun and wind as if by topiarists. The Great Topiarist of the Sky, I thought. There is a Divinity that shapes our ends, rough hew them how we will. Or words to that eff. . . .

Christ in Heaven, what was that? A shape precisely like a magpie but blue wings, blue tail, a blue so gentle yet brilliant it was like powdered sky, it rose up from near the roadside and floated with easy grace under the oily dark green of the oaks and then up and out of sight into the branches.

'Jo,' I said, as urgently as I could. I had to check while the vision was still strong in my eyes. 'Get the bird book. Look up magpies. What other birds are on the same page?'

'Siberian Jay, Jay, Azure-winged Magpie...'

'That's it. Read what it says.'

'Common but very local in its limited range (which represents a relic population as the main distribution is in China). Do you want the description?'

'Yes, yes.'

It fitted exactly.

'God, that was it. And, outside China, they only occur in Spain, right?'

'That's what the map indicates.'

'Oh boy. I must be sure. Let me see the picture. No, it's all right, I can just have a glance at it. All right, of course I can see him. Yes, look there's a sketch of it in flight...'

'Careful. CAREFUL!'

Too late.

Right up Saul's back-side. Crash!

Actually, it wasn't too bad at all. I had seen his brake lights, and although the shunt was loud we were both wearing seat belts and neither of us hit the windscreen which did not shatter. What I had not realised was that he had been slowing down for some time and so I had been edging nearer gradually. And what I did not know was why he had been slowing down.

A lorry had gone off the road in front of us and the Guardia Civil had set up one way traffic. At that moment the traffic had been the other way. Saul had stopped as the guardia waved him down. I had not. Simple as that.

CHAPTER IX

The Guardia Civil never seem to hurry, but they are never late. There was one at the window before I had even wound it down and I swear he hadn't run.

'It's a fair cop,' I began to blather, 'driving without due care and consideration...'

God, they frighten me, the guardias. And it's not just their awful reputation. They are so smooth, so slick, so neat. So efficient.

This one, a motor-cyclist and so helmeted rather than with the patent leather hat, pulled off his gauntlets, folded them on the regulation creases and tucked them in his glossy belt. Then, with strong but clean fingers, he undid his square pouch thing and produced his wad of forms and his pencil.

At this point Saul appeared at the other side and Jo started tugging at my sleeve. Distracted I turned away, appearing to ignore the guardia. He did not like that.

'Saul wants to know should he act angry or make nothing of it?' she whispered urgently.

'For Christ's sake, I don't know. Play it by ear.'

'*Pero bueno,*' said the guardia, '*usted está tonto. ¿Es qué no tiene ojos en la cara? ¿Cómo, es ciego?*'

'*Sí, sí,*' I said. He looked even more fed up.

'*¡Qué no se va a justificar con tales tonterías!*'

'Si, señor, si.'*

I could see something had gone wrong from his face.

'Where the hell is Del?' I cried.

Saul had decided, having I suppose a rotten ear, to play the angry stranger whose rear bumper had been done. He was enjoying it too.

'Look here. You've jolly well got to give your name, address, and insurance company. No excuse at all for bumping me, cost at least fifty quid to straighten that. You had plenty of warning.' And then I think he went a bit far. 'Dash it all, old chap,' he said, 'we must be British about it, eh what? I mean to say, fair play and all that. Show the Dago these things can be settled without knives and all that.'

At which Jo burst into fits of hysterical laughter.

I yelled at her to shut up; the guardia, who had also been saying something, thought I was shouting at him and unfastened the flap on his pistol holster. I seemed to be the only one of us who could see how fed up he was.

'Saul. Will you please get Del.'

At last she arrived.

'Mis amigos son ingléses. No hablan español. Pero yo si que hablo español,' she said, gently. Somehow she contrived the manner and appearance of the more fetching sort of madonna. The guardia calmed down a little and yammered away at her for about three minutes. At last he drew breath.

'He says he thinks you are mad. You are an imbecile. You have been abusive, too. This is a very serious matter. You ...'

But he was off again. The gestures were coming faster

* 'Well, well. We have a right one here. Don't you have eyes in your head? You must be blind.' 'Yes, yes.' 'You're not going to justify yourself with such idiocies.' 'Yes, sir, yes.'

125

now—the short prod with the forefinger towards Del's nose, the expressive shake of the loose wrist, the finalising karate chop.

'Both cars must be driven down to the police station. They will be impounded until all the evidence has been collected...'

Jo's hysterics changed swiftly from the major to the minor key.

'They'll search the van, they'll search he van,' she wailed.

I felt sick and dizzy. Fortunately Saul now recovered his senses.

'Tell him, Del,' he said slowly and firmly, 'tell him two things. One: we are all friends. The damage done to my van is purely a personal matter between us. I have no wish to take him to court and I shall not even report the accident to my insurance company.'

She said all that. The guardia started up in answer, but Saul got in quickly again.

'Two: We sleep in these vans. Obviously his enquiries will take a long time. It is very late. If he impounds the vans we will have nowhere to sleep. Hotels will be full or very expensive. Tell him we will drive to the Salamanca camp site. He can escort us if he likes. We will report to the police station tomorrow at whatever time he likes. He can take our passports as security.'

She did all that. By then I had recovered.

'Tell him,' I said, 'I plead guilty to driving stupidly. That I will make all possible reparations to my friend here. That my wife is very nervous and easily upset and any more strain could be...'

'Bloody hell,' cried Jo. 'Keep me out of it.' She stopped sobbing.

Del did it all marvellously. Gradually the guardia simmered down. He returned to his forms and his pencil.

'I think it's going to be all right,' Del murmured, and we went through the *nombre, domicilio, pasaporte* bit; and then the *matrícula, clase, categoría* of the vans. Finally he handed me his pad.

'Sign here,' Del said.

I signed. *Firma del Denunciado*—signature of the denounced. Oh dear. I looked at the heading. *Boletín de Denuncio*. It looked bad.

'He wants eight hundred pesetas fine.'

'Is that all?'

'I think so. Just a moment.' She rattled away at him. 'No, I'm afraid not. He's taking up Saul's suggestion. We're to go to the camp site and report to the *Jefatura Provincial de Tráfico* in Salamanca tomorrow at midday. He wants our passports.'

'They'll not let us into the camp site without them.'

'He's coming with us to the camp site.'

'Phew. OK. It could have been worse. Well done Del. Well done Saul.' And I forked out the eight hundred pesetas. 'Bloody Azure Winged Magpie.'

And so we made our triumphal entry into Salamanca. Well, not exactly. The camp site the guardia took us to is about three miles east of the town on the Madrid road; we were coming from the south, and got on to this road without crossing the Tormes which runs round the south side of the city. But we did get, for a mile or more, the most magnificent view of a city that I think I have ever seen. First through a curtain of poplars, then more clearly, and finally set above the twenty-six arches of the Roman bridge we saw the hills of the city, the university buildings, and the twin cathedrals, all lit by the last gleams of the setting sun and reflected in the wide, still Tormes, with swallows skimming above the mirrored images. And to cap it all and just as we were moving away down the Madrid road, floodlights came on on the bridges and all the main buildings.

The camp site seemed pleasant, set as it was, behind a large hotel some of whose amenities—bars, swimming pools, restaurant—it shared. It was on a slight slope planted with poplar saplings in tidy rows and hedged with privet. We settled in up in one far corner. Our guardia saluted and disappeared into the dusk with our passports.

All four of us shared the same reaction: we wanted a drink. We had several drinks. Rums and Coke mostly, as far as I remember. Saul insisted on cooking us a meal. He boiled up huge amounts of macaroni and tipped stewed minced meat, ketchup, and, if you please, tuna fish on it and said it was *Italiana*. It seemed a good reason for going down to the shop for a couple of bottles of *tinto*.

I remember that at one point he began to sing, to the tune of *We shall not be moved*:

> 'We were done by the fu-u-u-u-zz
> We were done by the fuzz, toda-a-a-a-y.'

and to the tune of *Blowing in the Wind*:

> 'What shall a man get who smashes up his van,
> What shall he get for this crime?
> The answer my friend is a bloody great fine,
> The answer my friend is a fine.'

The camp site broke out in to a babel of recrimination like the U.N. debating a vote of censure and we managed to make him shut it.

It seemed far too long before Del and I got into the blue van.

'Alone at last,' I breathed thickly in her ear, tugging at her jeans.

'There's bloody great ants,' shouted Saul, from outside. 'Bloody great, thick, black ants as big as my little finger.'

Del insisted that he came in. We tried it for a bit—I mean just sleeping, three in a five foot area, and I got fed up. But Jo had locked herself in the other van. I slept uneasily across the two front seats of the blue van and was woken at dawn by the sound of Saul and Del making love on the other side of the thin curtain.

CHAPTER X

Since most of the rest of what happened took place in or near Salamanca I think I should describe briefly the topography of the town. The old part, the part that matters, is shaped like a squashed semi-circle with the River Tormes providing the diameter in the south. The semi-circle is an inner ring road of avenues linked at more or less attractive modern squares; this marks the boundary of the old city. Outside there is the usual sprawl of apartment blocks, small factories and so on. Roughly in the middle of the old town is the Plaza Mayor—a large eighteenth-century porticoed square of remarkable beauty, the best in Spain. To the south and south-west of this lie the cathedrals, the main university buildings, several large churches and convents, and a small area of late mediaeval domestic building now run down and threatened with demolition. The area to the east of the Plaza is modern for the most part and is where most of the government offices, main post office and so on are. To the north is the commercial area dating mostly from the turn of the century. Nothing particularly exciting here, but it's pleasant enough. The whole city is built over three quite steep hills.

It has its place in English history. Nearby, four miles to the south, are Los Arapiles—two oddly shaped cliffs which rise from the undulating plain. Round these hills was fought, in 1812, the Battle of Salamanca when the then Lord Wellington inflicted a huge and decisive defeat on the French.

So much for the guide book bit.

Optimistically we packed up at about eleven o'clock next morning, expecting to be on our way to the north as soon as we had finished with the police. The *Jefatura de Tráfico* was on the ring road and turned out to be a dull Edwardian sort of building, dusty and run-down. We were there before twelve and were kept waiting for more than an hour before anything happened. Then an elderly officer was kind enough to tell us that nothing could be done that day since the papers had not been sent over from the Headquarters of the Guardia Civil.

'Couldn't we go over now and sort it out?' I asked, a suggestion that was quietly but firmly dismissed by the policeman.

'Come back tomorrow at twelve,' he said through Del. *Adiós, adiós*, all round.

Back to the camp site where we had a very embarrassed and expensive lunch by the swimming-pool. Saul and Del seemed to find difficulty meeting my eyes and I found I didn't much want to look at them anyway. We drank too much sangria and after a time Del and Jo went off to wash their own hair and everybody's smalls.

'Sorry about last night,' muttered Saul, sucking a slice of purple orange from the sangria jug. He giggled. 'And this morning.'

'I'm not going to hang one on you if that's what you're frightened of,' I said. 'Apart from anything else, I'm too bloody tired.'

We had a swim instead.

At five o'clock Jo and Del announced that they wanted fresh food for supper and that they weren't going to use the restaurant again. And anyway they wanted a change of scenery. Would I run them into town?

We all went in the orange van. I had some difficulty parking but in the end found a place near the Plaza. This suited me: I wanted a drink. The girls set off to do their shopping and Saul said he had some cards to post.

The Plaza cheered me up. Two sides of it have good cafés with tables right out into the square. It was crowded, of course, with hundreds of Americans—Salamanca is a centre for one of their summer language schools—and I had to wait a long time before a waiter showed any interest in me. But it didn't matter. The sun shone on the golden stone-work; pigeons rose, flapped listlessly and settled again on the cornucopias, swags, cupids and goddesses of the baroque town hall; sleek Spaniards with rich curly hair lounged with easy hauteur while their shoes were shined or made lazy gestures to their adoring American consorts.

I ordered a gin and tonic. The waiter carried the Gordon's (Málaga) bottle on his tray, the Sch..... tonic, and a tall, tall glass of ice and lemon. With fine leger-demain the Gordon's was sloshed into the glass, half-way, two thirds to the top, the cap lifted one-handed from the tonic, and the briefest gurgle to top up. Wait a moment for the ice to bite into the gin. Then ... bloody marvellous that drink was. By the time I was half way through it I had almost stopped worrying about the thirty-six thousand pounds' worth of hash in the unoccupied van and could even think of Saul and Del with a sort of equan-imity.

That night the sleeping arrangements returned to normal. That is, I slept in the company of, rather than with, Jo. The large black ants seemed to have terminated my intimacy with Del.

Next morning, back to the *Jefatura*. Our kind friend

132

there had news for us. Could Mr Elmer please report to
the Guardia Civil at four-thirty? There was no need for
anyone else to go—just Mr Elmer. There would be no
language problem, an adequate interpreter would be
present. The Casa Cuartel of the Guardia Civil was in
Plaza Colón, not far from the Plaza Mayor.

I drove the others back to the camp and we had lunch.
They set about amusing themselves in one way or
another, but I couldn't settle. As the afternoon moved on
and got hotter I began to feel more and more frightened
about the coming interview—like a schoolboy who has an
appointment with his headmaster before he goes home. I
drifted about the camp site and back to Del who was sun-
bathing, alone, near the vans. I squatted beside her.

'OK then?' she asked.

'Yes. I suppose so.'

'Say, Mark. I'm sorry about those ants.'

'So am I. There don't seem to be many around now.'

'I guess they get in out of the sun at this time of day. I
expect I should too.'

'Yes.'

'Mark. Put some oil on my back.'

I slowly rubbed the sun oil over her shoulders, round
her shell-like shoulder-blades, down into the small of her
back, where drops of sweat glistened.

'Mark?'

'Um?'

'Would you like to fuck? Saul and Jo are both swimming. We could use the proper bed in your van.'

Blood pounded about my ears and I felt sick.

'It's a quarter past three, Del. I'll never make it to the
Guardia Civil in time.'

'Oh, go on. We won't take long. And I feel all randy in
this heat.' Her hand was moving up my leg.

'Oh, Christ, yes. Come on.'

It was a very bright twilight in the curtained van and very hot. Sweat poured off both of us, sticking our skin together so that we made sucking, plopping sounds when my chest separated from her breasts. Her damp hair seemed to be everywhere; the odours of sweat, sex and sun oil were almost overpowering.

'Twenty to four.'

'Ten minutes at least before you need move.'

Her hand moving, teasing, gliding, artfully playing.

'No, Del, no!'

'Why not?'

'There's not time. It'll take longer this time.'

'You don't want to.'

'Of course I do but . . .'

'Well, then. Oh, come on.'

'No, Del. Del!' Green uniform. Boots. Forms. *Denuncio*. Pistol. 'I must go.' Green suitcases. Hashish. Ten years' Spanish jail. 'Del, I'm going.'

I pushed her away and reached for my clothes.

'You sod. I'll never fuck with you again.' Pause. 'I'll scream if you put those pants on.' Grabbing my shirt. 'I'll get out of the van just as I am and run all round the site waving this above my head.'

'Go on then,' suddenly irritated, 'I don't mind. I've got a clean one in the back.'

'You bastard!' She threw herself down, twisting her body across the bed, with her head in the pillow. I looked at my watch. Five past four already. I wasn't even sure if I could find my way there.

'Del. I'm going. In this van. And I don't really care whether you come or not. I'll count three, then I'm opening the curtains. One. Two. Three.'

I drew the front curtain from the windscreen which

134

was facing the hedge, then the one down the side opposite the blue van.

'Oh, all right. Fancy being so scared, shit-scared of the fuzz. Here, do my top up for me.'

She pulled on her bikini pants. Then, just as I was going to open the door for her, she made a grab at me and got hold of me, hard, well, you can guess where.

'Right,' she said and her voice was thick with laughter again, 'I've got you now. Just five more minutes and you'll be so late it won't be worth going.'

I hit her—not hard, but she was surprised enough to let go. Before she could retaliate I bundled her out, slammed the door, and got the engine going. As I moved I caught a glimpse of her in the rear-view mirror. With some nonchalance she was spreading herself out on the towel where I had found her.

There were still shocks to come. As I left the site a white Mini with Málaga registration plates was coming in—a fair-haired driver and a dark passenger. I couldn't be certain, they were wearing sun-glasses—but I felt pretty sure that Charley and Paco had arrived. I was sick, disgusted, frightened at the thought: it seemed that every time we got held up for more than a day—at Málaga, Granada, and now here—they would come homing in as if by some delayed telepathy, like wasps or birds of carrion. I wondered bitterly how long it would be before Chichester or the mysterious Mr Jones appeared.

And that, of course, was the second shock.

The traffic policeman's directions were, naturally, accurate and I had no trouble finding the Casa Cuartel of the Guardia Civil behind the Dueñas, an old monastery where Columbus studied the putative roundness of the world with certain learned monks. I parked the van—hash and all—in the inner courtyard, passed under the motto *Todo por la Patria*—which might as well have been *Lascia spera* the way I felt—and found an information desk. My identity was established and a young officer took me down a passage, knocked on a door, and showed me in.

For a moment I thought Columbus had been misled. The world was flat and I had fallen off. Sime was on the other side of the desk. Desperately I clutched at the only possible explanation.

'You must be the interpreter,' I blurted out.

'Pull your head in. I'm Detective Sergeant Simon Sands of the Metropolitan Police, seconded to the Central Drugs Intelligence Unit. Come in Mr Elmer, pull up a chair and rest your rosy cheeks.'

CHAPTER XI

It was a dim, cool room: the external blind was dropped over most of the open window. Beneath it I could make out a pleasant, green, tiny town garden filling an internal patio. Through the rows of holes between each slat the hot light poured making a pattern of elongated dots on the floor at my feet and on the desk at which Sime sat. As far as I could see—he was silhouetted against the light— he was just the same old Sime: curly blond hair, open-necked military shirt, shorts, beefy, hairy legs, exuding an atmosphere of cheery antipodean bonhomie. His accent remained the same. But the blue folded card that he pushed across to me seemed authentic enough—it was stamped on the outside with a familiar looking silver badge, on the inside there was a photograph and brief particulars declaring that, yes, the holder was indeed Detective Sergeant...

'I expect this comes as a bit of a surprise,' he said with a broad grin. Somehow or other, I don't remember how, I had arrived on a high-backed chair facing him.

'Yes, it does.' The sun glanced through a beaker of water on the desk. 'Could I have a drink?'

'Sure. I'm sorry there's only water.' He poured it out and it gurgled as refreshingly as the water Moses struck from the stone in Sinai or wherever. It was quite cold to taste too. 'Right, Mr Elmer, I think we had better get down to business. I don't mean to seem ill-disposed towards you but I should judge that the new footing on which we are now established demands a return to more formal modes of address. So—*Mister* Elmer, and you may call me Officer or Mister Sands.'

Have you noticed how ex-colonial speakers of English become all pompous when they are embarrassed?

'Just as you say—er, Mr Sands.'

'Good,' as if to a pupil who has learnt his first lesson well. 'Now. Mr Elmer, you have in your possession, most probably in the van outside, somewhere between twenty and a hundred kilos of hashish. Yes?'

'About thirty, I believe.' The words were a dull croak. I reached for the water again. Sweat was pricking my eyes, the back of my throat was sore, I felt an awful emptiness in my stomach.

'Here in Spain,' he said, but of course it was 'Spine', 'that could get you up to ten years. In England, first offence, respectable background, you might, with a good lawyer, get off with six. Say two off for remission and at least two in a good open prison like Ford, Sussex, adds up to indicating that it would be better for you (yew) if we made the arrest in England.'

I must keep reminding you that all this was said with him tilting his chair back, resting his hairy athlete's knees on the edge of the desk, and with a great big smile. One thing I will say for Simon Sands—he enjoys his work.

'But in return for not handing you over to my very good friends and colleagues in the Guardia Civil, here in Salamanca, I shall of course expect some co-operation. What I think a pommie ... excuse I, what I think you would call a *quid pro quo*.'

This sudden flash of erudition did not cheer me up at all.

138

'Of course,' I croaked.

'But first let me recapitulate. You were meant to take this hash with your lady (lidy) wife, who isn't your wife and may be no ... least said, eh? Excuse I ... on the package tour plane back to London, where in return for not very much money, you would hand it over to its owner, Michael Chichester. Right?'

By now I could only nod.

'But you were greedy and you decided to keep the hash and make much more money for yourself. You assumed, I suppose, that Chichester would not be able to do much about it without incriminating himself.'

Another nod.

'You may well have been right. Of course, he could have given you concrete shoes and dropped you in the Thames, but I doubt if he's quite that class of crook. But that's by the way.'

He started to fiddle with a pen. Collecting his thoughts, I suppose.

'To that end, you fixed up this whole trip with two vans and three accomplices, to hijack the hash and bring it up through Spain and France, to England. Or were you going to use the Bilbao-Southampton ferry?'

'No, you see Jo is easily sea ...'

'It's of no material importance.' For a moment he sounded almost bored. 'Then things went wrong. You were held up at Málaga. By the time you left not only Chichester was on to you, but Charley and Paco, and of course yours truly (trewly). Mr Elmer, has it ever occurred to you to ask why?'

'Why what?' I croaked, then cleared my throat. 'Oh, I see what you mean. No. I mean, I just assumed that they were all very interested in the hash, and the delay at Málaga gave you all time to get on our trail. I thought you were working for Chichester.'

'Why ever did you think that?' For a moment he was surprised. 'Never mind. It's of no material importance. Mr Elmer, if you want to believe that, there's no reason why you shouldn't. But I know how my old acquaintances Charley and Paco manage to keep in touch with you.'

Numbly I remembered the Málaga Mini. Was Jo right about Del after all?

'Incidentally, yours truly has been interested in you since your trip to Kew Gardens last April, but even so I should have lost you twice, maybe three times, but for the offices of my good friends in the Guardia Civil. But none of this has material importance.' Suddenly he lowered his knees and let the front legs of his chair hit the floor with a bang that was echoed by his golden hands slapping the desk. 'But this has. Chichester is fairly big stuff—clever and slippery. Through you we might be able to catch him in England with hash in his possession. That would be nice. But I can think of something nicer. Do you know who Charley and Paco work for?'

'Mr Jones, is it? Someone who doesn't like Chichester. They're in Salamanca. I saw them on the way here.'

'Too right. They work for Mr Jones who is the Mr Big of the cannabis trade. And, you know what, Mr Elmer? The gentleman I refer to is right here in Salamanca, too. Now normally he wouldn't bother with a medium-sized load like yours—he has his own channels. But Chichester has annoyed him. Probably because Chichester, who has mostly supplied the telly and theatrical end of the market has recently been undercutting Mr Big on the campuses. I think Mr Big believes he can use this situation that has arisen because of you to chop Chichester in little pieces for good and all. But, of course, he's exposing himself, too. And with luck, and your help, we can get him put away as well as Chichester, and that would be fair dinkum.'

He said this with great relish—as if the idea was a huge T-bone steak covered with mushrooms and onions.

'I see,' I said. I wasn't too sure if I did: I had had too many shocks and a terrible weariness had settled on me. The sun flashed from the fluttering wings of sparrows outside. I caught myself trying to remember the difference between them and the English variety. I made an effort. 'What do you want me to do?'

'Well, Mr Elmer. Ideally I would like you to light out of Salamanca like a bat out of hell and head for England as fast as possible, and hope Chichester and Mr Jones...'

'That can't be his real name...'

Impatient gesture as if brushing away a fly.

'Of course not. Hope that they will tag along all the way to Blighty without doing anything until we all get there together. Then I could bust them where I want them, against a legal system I know. However, the fact that Mr Jones himself is here suggests he is planning for something to happen here in Spain—something which will destroy Chichester and leave him the hash. In other words, I doubt if you'd get very far out of Salamanca. Especially not now Charley and Paco have located you.' His hand brushed his rib cage where Paco's knife had scarred him. His voice took on a meditative tone. 'That Paco's a fucking bastard—drongo from Paraguay or some such bastard place.' He chirped up again. 'But, if you sit tight on the camp site and in the town for a day or two they won't be able to do much, and Mr Jones will have to take the initiative. He'll try to proposition you and when he does, we'll know what he's up to. So. Here is what you do—'

He leant forward over the desk; a gold identity disc dropped from his shirt front and dangled in front of him

—no, not a disc, a star of David, would you believe it?
'—You go back to the camp and let it be known that the Guardia Civil haven't decided what to do with you yet. Let me see. Today's Thursday. And that you have to report back here at midday on Saturday. Meanwhile I shall keep out of sight. That's one advantage we have: they still think I'm in hospital in Seville with a perforated lung. So they think they have time on their side. And on Saturday you'll report here to me and we'll be able to decide on the next step, according to what's happened to you in the meantime.'

That 'we' stirred something in me.

'Er, Mr Sands—why do I have to do this? I mean why don't I just take the hash out of the van and drop it in the River Tormes?'

He leant back. grinning, and popped his star back into his shirt.

'Interesting question, Mr Elmer. And the answer to it raises another point. The Spanish police are very interested in you, because of me, because of Málaga, your crash and so on. They know you're smuggling something, and coming out of Tangiers they're pretty sure they know what. But because I'm working with them and I've promised them that Mr Jones, who has been pushing cannabis on Spanish campuses, will be busted either here or in England, they've agreed not to pull you in. But believe me, they're never very far from you, and I reckie that if you tried to ditch your hash you'd suddenly find the landscape full of green uniforms. Ten years, Mr Elmer, is a mighty long time.'

CHAPTER XII

Mr Jones turned out to be rather out of the ordinary and he was in touch very soon too. I suspect that Charley and Paco had found out from one or other of my 'friends' at the camp site where I was, and were waiting for me outside the Guardia Civil headquarters. They then followed me up to the Plaza, saw me firmly stuck into a gin and tonic, and reported back to their boss who was, naturally enough, staying at the Gran Hotel, just off the Plaza.

I was sitting there trying to collect myself after the shock I'd had—turning over all sorts of unpleasant thoughts from the apparent near certainty of a jail sentence in either England or Spain to the thought of going back to the camp where I could no longer trust anyone, including Del. Not that that specifically mattered any more—I doubted if she would sleep with me again after the thump I'd given her. Yet, such is human nature, I could still enjoy a certain hot sweatiness in a certain area and the recollections that went with it.

'The egregious Mr Elmer, I presume.'

I do hate people who use words they don't understand. No one really knows what 'egregious' means.

'May I join you?' The voice was almost lost in the flinty throatiness some chain-smokers develop in later life. I hope I won't be misunderstood if I mention the late

W. H. Auden in this connection: there was no other point of similarity at all between them. I looked up.

He was short, almost small; of indeterminate age, but certainly well over sixty; dressed immaculately in an un-patterned brown suit, cream shirt, slim shoes that shone like mirrors. On his head was a brown hat, a derby I believe they used to be called, very wide brimmed with the brim turned up at the front. His face was pale, very much lined, and very very clean. Like a newly washed corpse. He wore gold-rimmed spectacles and carried a gold-knobbed cane and smoked through a gold-mounted holder. I might not have guessed who he was had I not seen Paco hovering protectively near at hand.

'Er, yes. That's right. Can I, er, get you something to drink?'

But he was already sitting opposite me and the waiter, who had left customers in mid-sentence to attend him, was at his side. He spoke fluent Spanish, with many gestures implying exactness, precision in support of his order. The waiter nodded, bowed, and yes, scraped with 'Claro, señor', and 'Sí, señor', and 'Como usted quiera, señor'.

'The ordinary Spanish don't really understand sherry and one has to be very careful when ordering; have you found that? I'm so sorry. My name is—shall we say Jones?'

Gentleman Jones. Paco was now propping up a pillar behind us.

The waiter brought an unopened bottle of dry sherry and ceremoniously poured a little into a small wine glass. The sun shone through it and it glowed almost exactly to match the pale topaz in Mr Jones's cuff-link.

'Quite passable.'

He sat still for about five minutes except to dab at the

144

corner of a rheumy eye which had begun to run and to give a tiny circular wave of his hand to a passer-by who ostentatiously doffed his hat to him.

'The manners of the *paseo*—such a fine old-world custom, don't you think, Mr Elmer?'

'You seem to be known here, Mr Jones.' It was all I could think of saying.

'I have acquaintances in many places, Mr Elmer. A fine web of relationships covering much of the western world. I travel a deal.'

He coughed politely behind his hand, drew out a gold spike from some inner pocket and levered the butt from his cigarette holder.

'Did you have a satisfactory outcome with the guardias just now?' he asked.

Fortunately I kept my head.

'Fairly. They still want me to report back on Saturday.'

'We must see what we can do to stop them from bothering you.'

He took another cigarette from a tortoiseshell case; it was lit—by the obsequious waiter. At last the ritual was completed.

'You met Charley and Paco in Ventleigh, I think, so you have some idea of whom I am. And I gather you saw them at work for me in Seville cathedral. The object of their attentions on that occasion—the young and conscientious Sands—is making a slow recovery in the police infirmary of that town. Did you know young Sands was an English bobby?'

Again I kept my head—an achievement under the circumstances. It was nice to see that Mr Jones was rather far from infallibility.

'No. Really?' I said with finely simulated surprise. 'I thought he was Australian.'

'He is, dear chap. Was doing rather well with the Sydney force but ran into some racial prejudice amongst the red necks. He's a Semite you know. Apparently he argued that since these people had come from London because they found the racial mix a bit strong for them there, that city might be the place for him.' He sipped his sherry, sucked in smoke through his holder and breathed it out into the golden sunlight. 'I mention all this to remind you that I am a man with resources, so you will want to listen to what I have to say. Mr Elmer, you are in a fix, a fix of your own making. I could do any number of things to you to punish you for continuing to associate with Chichester after my warning in April—I could let Charley and Paco have their way with you again; I could pick up your cargo at any time to suit my convenience; or I could simply ring up the guardias and let them find it. However, I prefer to use you.' That eye was running again and had to be dabbed. 'Also I admire your enterprise in trying to run off with Chichester's consignment and, while naturally I won't let you have the full value, I think I might pay you a couple of thousand for your trouble in bringing it so far. Are you interested?'

I nodded. I didn't trust myself to speak.

'Good. Here is what you do. I want you to make contact with Chichester—not the other way round, that's important. You will tell him that because of my presence and that of Charley and Paco you have decided to give him back his hash. But, you will say, you are under close observation much of the time, and so he will have to follow your instructions.'

He coughed and again pulled out his gold spike, cleared his holder, and again the waiter was ready with his lighter. I took the opportunity to interrupt.

'How do I get in touch with Chichester?' I asked.

For a moment he looked surprised.

'Through Jo Tangmere, of course. It must be she who is double-crossing you with him, don't you think?' The full implications of this did not hit me immediately, and I allowed him to continue. 'On Sunday, at Alba de Tormes, there is a bull fight; a *novillada* only, but with quite a likely looking lad performing. You will go, with all your friends. After the *banderilla* of the third bull you will go out to your van and you will hand over to him there the two suitcases. That is all, Mr Elmer.'

And quite suddenly he was off. Paco was at his side helping him up, he touched the brim of his hat with his cane and there he was, dapper, neat, but just a shade unsteady, trotting across the Plaza to the far corner and the Gran Hotel.

I paid the bill. His sherry cost fifty pesetas, which was ridiculous.

I knew too much now and I could not bring myself to return to the camp site, straightaway. I drifted down the Rua Mayor towards the cathedrals, passed blindly in front of the extraordinary west door, and came to a small enclosed square which seemed to exist as a forecourt to the one building with steps and a balcony. Headquarters of Generalissimo Franco during the Civil War, a notice read. I shuddered, and made my way back by a slightly different route and came upon the magnificent baroque façade of the Clerecía beneath its lovely twin towers. I sat on the warm steps for a few moments looking at the strange wall of the Casa de las Conchas inset with rows of carved stone shells. My thoughts began to clear.

Jo was spying on me for Chichester. I wondered why. Surely she could not expect anything like the sort of money she would have got with me, but perhaps after all she had decided that he had a more certain market than I. So much for her attacks on Del—they must have been a blind to distract me from suspecting her. Well, that explained how Chichester had got on to us. But what about Mr Jones himself, and his two heavies? Jo was surely not spying for both sides ... Oh Christ, I thought and stood up. So that's why Del went to bed with me. The first time was on the very evening when I had suggested that we ought to split up. I gritted my teeth and started walking again. And that would explain her sudden passion for me this afternoon. Yes. I could see it now. Gentleman Jones's plan obviously depended on my not seeing Chichester before I had been told what to do; so Del had been instructed to keep me on the camp site, and preferably in a van, until Charley and Paco had caught up again.

I felt the sort of hurt a child feels when some cherished illusion is shattered, in public, to the sound of unthinking laughter. I was lost too. I was in another small square with a pleasant bit of grass and three good trees shading a Rodinesque statue of the philosopher Miguel de Unamuno. I remembered. Rector of Salamanca University. Made an anti-fascist speech here, in the Nationalist camp, shortly before he died. As a philosopher had been much concerned with problems of personal identity. Well, I knew how he felt.

Christ. What was I to do? How could I go back and face those two harpies?

I was now quite a long walk from the Plaza de Colón where I had left the van, a walk which went through the Plaza Mayor again and past about twenty other bars apart from the ones there. I was quite drunk when I got back and it was just getting dark.

CHAPTER XIII

I can see the scene in my mind even now, quite vividly. Saul had rigged up a hurricane lamp in the doorway of the blue van and he was sitting on the step peeling potatoes. Del, dressed now, was sitting on a cushion with a glass in her hand, and Jo was in the driver's doorway next to Saul. They looked a pleasant, even happy group—English campers on holiday. The cosiness of it added bile to my bitterness.

I parked leaving about five yards between the vans, turned out the lights and jumped down.

Saul looked up, his glasses reflected the light from his lamp, and I noticed that his chin was bristly. It must have been days since he shaved.

'Hi!' he called. 'Where have you been? We were getting quite worried about you. Del thought she'd made you late and that you'd been put in prison for it.'

She came up—a huge smile lighting her face.

'Honey, it's true—I really was worried out of my mind ... honey, what's up?'

I raised my hand to hit her. She interpreted the movement correctly—I think the others did, too. Saul almost ran to her side and Jo stood up.

'You're not still mad at me are you?'

'He's mad all right,' said Saul.

'Drunk too, by the look of it,' said Jo.

'All right,' I said and my arm dropped. 'Saul, come with me. I want to talk to you on your own.' And I turned on my heel.

He followed me up the slope to the end of the camp site. I pushed heedlessly through the thin hedge and jumped a ditch. We were in a wide stony field of stubble on the side of a low hill. I walked up it until we were well above the site and then sat down. Saul sat beside me.

'Saul. I've had enough.'

He nodded, sympathetically and sensibly.

'Those women are bitches.'

Still he said nothing.

'You know Charley and Paco are about, don't you? They followed me into town. Chichester will be around soon. You see?'

'You're under a lot of strain,' he began.

'Shit, no. Look, I know what I'm talking about. Look, I know. Jo is in touch with Chichester, probably by post to prearranged poste restante addresses I should think; so it has to be Del who tipped off Charley and Paco and...' —I was about to say 'Gentleman Jones'—'...and other gentlemen.' Some instinct for survival, or perhaps just downright paranoia stopped me. I suddenly didn't want even Saul to know about either of my meetings that afternoon.

'Well anyway, I've had enough,' I went on. 'I want to get shot of the hash—Chichester seems to be the right person to have it. You give this message to Jo for me, will you? She's to go to Chichester and tell him I'll meet him outside the bull ring at Alba de Tormes on Sunday during the third bull fight. And I'll give him back his suitcases and all his hash then.'

'Why don't you tell her yourself?'

'Sorry, Saul. I just can't face either of them now. I feel

so sick of the whole thing. I just want to go to bed and forget about it all.' I could feel tears pricking now.

'OK, I'll tell her.' He scooped up a handful of stones and started tossing them one by one down the slope.

'Where are you going to sleep?'

'Oh, I don't know. Out on the ground. You did.'

'There really are ants here. Look, I think you're in pretty bad shape and you ought to have a proper rest. Why don't you book into the hotel at the camp site for a couple of nights?'

Suddenly the thought of a proper bed, of running hot water, of a room to myself seemed unbearably like the new Jerusalem.

'Yes, I think you're right. I'll do that, Saul.'

He stood up and his ridiculous hat was silhouetted against the orange rising moon. He gave me a hand.

'You're a good mate, Saul,' I added. 'It has all become a bit of a bloody nightmare.'

Alba de Tormes is about twenty kilometres south-east of Salamanca and is reached by a fairly straight minor road that cuts across the hills and through the ilex forest that separates the two towns. The drive is an attractive one—first the wheat plain undulates like a huge heaving sea broken by rocky outcrops. Two of the most extraordinary of these soon appear on the right—Los Arapiles where Wellington thrashed Marmont. Then comes the ilex forest and at about half way the Fuente de Santa Teresa—a spring that gushes beneath a banal figure of the saint. Finally the road drops through the hills to the town which is set inside a sweeping curve of the river amongst poplars and water meadows which continue on for many miles—an extended oasis between the parched hills and the oak forests. The small town is dominated by a ruined fortification dating

151

from the time when the Dukes of Alba were still interested in it, and has several churches and convents in one of which Saint Teresa of Ávila is buried, and in honour of whom the festival we were attending was celebrated.

I was in a fairly cheerful mood as I followed Saul and the blue van down to the long bridge: I had had a reasonably relaxing time for two days and I now felt that I could face whatever was to come.

I had not in fact gone to the hotel. Jo and Del had found too many drawbacks to that plan—Jo did not want to be left alone with the hash, Del pointed out that no hotel would accept me in the state that I was in, and so on—and so we had reached a compromise. Once they had really satisfied themselves that I had meant what I said about how they were spies for Chichester *et al*, they had realised that it would be better if we kept at a distance from each other. Jo and Del slept on the floor of the blue van and I had been put to bed in the orange one. Saul came in with me and slept across the front seats; to make himself more comfortable he filled the gap with the green suitcases.

I had stayed in bed all Friday and right through until twelve o'clock on Saturday and no doubt the rest did me good. I had been bothered at times by the sound of whispering outside, and Jo, once, came rummaging un-necessarily through my stuff. I couldn't see what she hoped to find that might interest Chichester. She rather rudely told me she was looking for dirty washing. Del, too, made one or two seductive moves, but quickly realised that she had ceased to be attractive to me now that I had recognised her duplicity. Saul continued kind and attentive.

But I suppose what had contributed most to my recovery was my second interview with Detective Sergeant Sands. He had decided that I should definitely go ahead with

Jones's plan of passing the hash over to Chichester at Alba. Obviously he reckoned on catching them both with the stuff later. And furthermore he had pointed out to me that once I had got rid of it, it would be very much more difficult for him or the Spanish police to charge me with smuggling. He added too that the Guardia Civil were no longer interested in the crash—the eight hundred peseta fine had cleared the record. I wondered if the long arm of Mr Jones was behind this minor reprieve. So, even though the girls were apparently now so frightened of me that both wanted to travel with Saul in the blue van, I really did think things were picking up. Saul had assured me that Jo had told him that Chichester would be at Alba and although I felt a bit nervous about the coming transaction I still felt that all my worries might well be over in a matter of three hours or so.

The town was crowded, even the bridge across was crammed with cars and young people trying to walk four or five abreast; there was a small fair with bumper cars at the bottom of the hill on the other side; firecrackers exploded and an open car, gaudily painted and filled with students playing musical instruments, went by. We had arrived over two hours early: this was to make sure we found a parking space near the bull ring and, in fact, we managed to achieve just this. Saul led the way through the narrow side streets up the hill and round the back of the fortress, almost as if he knew the way, and there, with a space behind it, parked opposite one of the main entrances, was the white Seat 1200 we had last seen on top of the hill at Estepa. No wonder Chichester had been in such a hurry to leave us then—once he had seen Sands approaching us. I backed into the gap, got out and waited while Saul found another place for the blue van.

It was nearly five minutes before he reappeared and I

passed the time tidying up the back of the van: suitcases near the front where they would be easy to get at; bed-clothes, can of spare petrol, and so on, between the rear seats; a large empty Coke bottle rolled out—but there was money on it and so I dropped it back in.

Saul was alone.

'Where are the girls?' I asked.

'They preferred to stay in the van. They've sent me to get tickets, then they're talking about getting some lunch or a sandwich.'

'Where do we get them?'

'The tickets? Over there perhaps,' and he gestured towards a small crowd milling around a black sedan at the top of a side-street. Oddly enough he was right—a couple of rather seedy men were sitting inside selling tickets while three guardias looked on benevolently. They were all the same price—seventy-five pesetas.

'I hope those guardias aren't around later,' I said.

'Not likely. Like every one else in Alba they'll be inside once it starts.'

'I hope you're right. What's the time?'

'Just gone two.'

'Right. Nearly two hours. I'll come with you for lunch.'

'Do you think that's wise? You've kept out of the girls' way since you found out about them very well up to now, but do you really think you'll be able to sit across the table from them for over an hour without starting some sort of row?'

'Oh, OK.'

He patted me sympathetically on the arm.

'Soon be over, old chum. Chin up. I'll meet you here at a twenty to four. Right?'

And off he sauntered—flared jeans swinging over his broken down training shoes, denim shirt with top pockets bulging with cigarettes, and that hat.

I wandered back into the town, feeling rather lonely, and found a restaurant which still had an empty seat or two. I ordered a *combinado*, a plate with three or four different dishes on—in this case rice, veal, omelette and Russian salad—and a half of wine—but I ate it quickly. The festival atmosphere was getting on my nerves: the customers, nearly all young, were banging on the tables, wine was spilt, raucous singing broke out. With nearly an hour to go I paid up and left.

Soon I found myself in the main square—an attractive place with a rose garden and palms in the middle, quite small but with wide balconies supported on thin cast-iron pillars, and a pleasant brick church. Here too of course there was a crowd, but there was more room and one was not constantly jostled.

'Hey, Mr Elmer.' I looked up. One of the balconies supported a restaurant or café. Del was leaning over, Jo by her side. I couldn't see Saul.

'Hey, Mr Elmer, won't you come up?' She looked marvellous, just as she always did, her hair falling down to frame her pert face. Her expression was completely open, so sincerely happy to see me it seemed, that I felt choked by anguish and bile to think of what she had done. I managed to make some sort of negative gesture. Saul had been right: I could not have faced them through a whole meal.

'Oh, come on, Mr Elmer.'

Jo leaned over too. 'Mark. Will we see you after the bull fight?'

My neck was aching, I was right below them—not more than a few feet separated us.

'Of course. It'll all be over then, won't it? I mean we won't have to worry about Chichester or anyone.'

She frowned, looked puzzled.

'Are you sure you're all right, Mark?'

That I think is the most irritating question anyone can ask.

'Of course I am.' And I walked on down the hill.

I stood watching the bumper cars for a bit and then walked out on to the bridge where I stood looking over the balustrade, and smoked. It was a pleasant scene. There was a wooded island below me and small pleasure boats, *pedalos*, you know the sort of thing, cruised over the almost still water. The festival was distant, less harsh. Funny, Del asking me up, I thought. She surely must have known how I felt about her. I turned and walked back towards the town and, as I did, a large American car, a chocolate coloured Ford Galaxy which almost spanned the bridge, came purring down towards me. Automatically I raised my hand in salute and Charley and Paco, who was driving, both grinned back from the front seats. Like tolerant royalty Mr Jones raised his cane in the back.

At the end of the bridge I could see Saul's bushwacker hat moving through the crowd up the hill in front of me. I called and caught him up.

CHAPTER XIV

The Alba bull ring is very small indeed: a simple cylinder of whitewashed brick and concrete about thirty feet thick; on the outside twenty feet high and on the inside ten feet. Inside there is a low parapet and then thirty feet of very rough terracing to the back wall. Apart from the spectators' entrance on to this terrace there is a large gate above which there is a rough, enclosed area with a roof and a wooden balcony—the president's box; on the other side, opposite, are two bolted metal doors for the entry of the bulls. The ring itself had been sanded over for the occasion, but not enough to hide the fact that grass and weeds had grown there undisturbed for nearly twelve months. Three of the *burladeros* were concrete slabs; the others, in contrast, were rotten and shaky.

After picking up the girls from the square we made our way together up on to the terrace. All the local *machos*—youths determined to demonstrate their manliness—already filled the parapet, sitting on it with their legs dangling into the ring, but we found a good view-point immediately behind them.

'Better stay fairly near the exit,' Saul whispered and I agreed, though it meant staying in the sun—a factor Jo pointed out.

'You know I must stay near the exit,' I said.

Again she looked puzzled, and then shrugged as if

giving up a difficult but unimportant problem.

The spaces around and behind us began to fill up quickly now: there were old men in black berets, and their black shawled wives; younger women with babes in arms; boys —not old enough to sit on the parapet, but old enough to snap gum and smoke cigarettes behind cupped palms; and girls in jeans with bouncy long, black hair, who, secure in groups of four or five, boldly back-chatted the *machos*. A band—two clarinets or fifes, and a couple of drums struck up a *paso doble* and the big gate to the street swung open. Gentry in very smooth pale suits and with highly polished bald heads took their places in the box—one of them, he would be the president of the fiesta, gave a nod.

From the street where it had been forming entered the *paseo*—but awkwardly. The problem was that they were entering from under the president's box, and since one of the purposes of the *paseo* is the bull fighters' salute to the president, they were in a fix—the first thing the president would see of them would be their back-sides. After a moment the elder of the matadors—'El Miura of Salamanca' the posters billed him as—sorted out the situation and they moved forward in as wide a sweep as possible beneath the dangling feet of the *machos*, before wheeling and coming down the middle. They halted more or less together, made their bows, the mules with yoke and chains disappeared through the great gate and— descending scale te-ta te-ta te-ta te-ta from the fifes—the iron door opened and out came the first bull.

He looked rather small. This was a *novillada*, a fight with young bulls and *novilleros*, trainee bull fighters. There would be only four fights, the bulls would be between two and three years old instead of five, there would be no *picador*, no man on a padded horse with a lance. But the bull, small though he was, was lively enough—fast, heavy-shouldered, wide-horned. He went round the ring like an express train and emptied it in two seconds flat. A deep and excited cheer rose from the crowd.

Enter El Miura, with the cape. His 'lights' were bottle green and gold, he was about twenty-two, very fit, very confident. He spun the bull around him three or four times, finally bringing it up sharp and panting. The crowd cheered again and he walked away from it, trailing the cape, one arm thrown up. He came and leant on one elbow on the *barrera* below us and chatted nonchalantly to the admiring *machos* above him while the members of his *cuadrilla* worked the bull some more. Naturally—they were not unmindful of who paid them—the bull gave them far more trouble than it had El Miura. It pawed the cape off one, and chased another, an overweight, middle-aged character behind a *burladero*. He made a bit of a show of squeezing in, which pleased the crowd.

Te-ta te-ta te-ta te-ta from the fifes. Time for the *banderillas*. El Miura was now playing the crowd more than the bull. He took two of the barbed darts and, holding them firmly at both ends, smashed them across the barrier, thus reducing the length of the shaft by more than half. He would have to let the bull get very close to be sure of fixing them properly, and the crowd would be merciless after a gesture like that if he failed.

The crowd fell quiet. Suddenly the bull ring seemed very small. The bull had returned to his station not far from the iron door. El Miura began to move across his vision, the hooves pawed, the head tossed, a cape fluttered from behind a barrier to confuse him, and then he came. El Miura timed his own run with dynamic geometry to cross the bull's path a yard in front of him and—ah! they were in and he was away with both hands above his head as the crowd rose, and the bull tossed and fretted to free its neck of the barbs.

With further barbs placed with similar elegance the bull's head began to drop and a silky sheen of crimson coursed down his shoulder. Again the fifes, and El Miura changed the cape for the *muleta* and sword, and dropped his hat in the dust behind him—dedicating the bull to us all.

I don't think he was in danger any more—the bull, young as he was, had slowed down a lot, but he was a game bull, as brave as you'll see and El Miura made the most of him. He worked him with incredible concentration, his eyebrows beetled, his face contorted into a frown of perfect absorption: it was the expression you sometimes see on the face of a pianist at the climax of a cadenza. I'm sure he had forgotten the crowd. He did not humiliate the bull: he could have twisted it over on to the ground, caught him by the horn, pulled his tail—I've seen all those done to please the crowd—but he let him come, always the bull came, and slowly the crowd caught the rhythm and the groundswell of 'olé' began to rise and fall like waves breaking on a beach.

At last the bull stumbled, seemed to go down on one knee. He had returned again to his station near the iron door, and he was panting, flanks heaving, tongue swollen. El Miura took the sword and sighted, shook the short cape and stamped his feet. But the bull would not come. It was perhaps the matador's only mistake—he had left the bull too long, he would no longer run on the sword and El Miura had to bring the sword to him.

The kill was not quite perfect. A rush of blood exploded over the bull's tongue and spilt into the sand, but then, as El Miura waved back his men who were coming up for the *descabello*, the knees finally caved and the eyes glazed.

The tiny ring burst into blossom, it seemed, as hundreds and hundreds of handkerchiefs fluttered to the rolling cheers of the crowd, and El Miura began his slow tour. It rained money, purses, flowers, leather bottles, black berets; a *macho* in front of us stripped off his shirt and threw that down. El Miura strutted from point to point, drank water or wine from the skins with head thrown back, legs splayed wide, and then with a wide backhanded sweep sent the skin, still spilling its wine as the bull had spilt its blood, skimming low over the heads of the crowd. They brought him the ears, and the mules, managing quite a canter even in that small ring, dragged off the carcass.

My last memory of that fight is of El Miura standing near the spot where the bull had died, holding a lady's handbag in outstretched hand. I can't think of any other situation where a man would not look so ridiculous.

'Woweeee,' sighed Del. 'And he's just a beginner?'

'I'm sorry,' said Jo, 'I'm too near. I didn't like it.' And she pushed her way to the very back wall, overlooking the road, as far from the ring as she could get.

The next bull was bigger and stronger; the matador, smaller, far less experienced and far younger—perhaps no more than seventeen. It soon became clear that he was frightened too—he could not let the bull get near him; yet there was a sort of grit—he had to hold on, he had to stay there, he had to see it through. I suppose that in Madrid or even in Salamanca, the crowd would have lacerated him —but they were not as unpleasant as they might have been, perhaps because in that small ring they could sense the young lad's agony—the dreadful fight, not with the bull, but with his fear. Perhaps they spared him because he was a local.

It was painful to watch and I found my eyes were scanning the crowd around us. Saul must have felt a similar impulse.

'Hey,' he said. 'Isn't that Chichester?' He pointed obliquely across an arc of the ring. 'Look. See the character in a red shirt on the parapet. To the left of him.'

It was Chichester all right. That black hair, the glossy skin were echoed around him, but his height and a sort of public school arrogance in his stance singled him out.

So he was here. And Mr Jones and his henchmen were around too: I wondered if Chichester had seen them. I shivered in the sunlight—like jackals or hyenas they were gathering for the moment when those green suitcases would be moved, and when the move was made I was to be there, right in the middle of it. Only one person was missing—Sime, Detective Sergeant Sands. Suddenly I realised that I wanted, needed him to be there. Under the strain my imagination stumbled childishly: if only he would appear in the uniform of a London policeman, helmet and all, then all would be well.

Some of the crowd had begun a slow handclap. This second bull was taking a long time. Desperately the young lad sighted the sword, and the bull came for him, hard and sudden, with a vicious hook of the horn; the sword flew out of his hand on impact, caught the sun and landed in the sand. I longed for it to be over—but on the second attempt I felt a sudden rush of relief as not only the bull but I too was reprieved.

'What's the matter, Mark?' Del mouthed through the crowd's derision.

'Nothing. I just wish it was all over.'

She squeezed my hand. The bull was on its knees but would not die. One of the *cuadrilla* stabbed at its neck with the wicked heavy knife they use for the *coup de grâce*. The head collapsed between its front legs and the crowd booed.

Enter the mules again—and this time they took the carcass round the ring and the crowd cheered the death of so strong and courageous a beast. The lad looked relieved —it was a compliment to him too, a sop to his pride. Chichester had gone. Without my noticing he had slipped away to keep our rendezvous.

And now this was it. The third bull, my bull. In he came, the dust flew, he looked big. El Miura spun the cape and the beast skidded and almost went over, and the crowd groaned—a fool of a bull, an insult to a good fighter. I waited for two or three minutes and then moved off, as unobtrusively as I could, towards the exit. Poor bull though it was, El Miura was doing everything he could to make a fight of it and everybody's eyes remained glued to him, hardly acknowledging my apologies as I went past.

I paused in the narrow archway of the spectators' entrance and lit a cigarette, gagged on it, and threw it away. I crossed the empty sunlit street towards my van and the Seat thirty yards away and every step I felt like a straw version of Gary Cooper in *High Noon*. Now I could see the Seat was still empty—where the hell was he? My scalp pricked. I drew near the van, began to dawdle. This was ridiculous. I felt in my pocket for a handkerchief since suddenly sweat was in my eyes, and my throat hurt.

A shadow moved behind me—I had walked right past the doorway he was in without seeing him.

'Well, well, well, Mr Elmer.' I think I had forgotten his voice—deepish, slow—did I say it was like Clement Freud's? Perhaps, a bit, but now with an icy menace the M.P. for wherever it is would never be able to emulate. I turned round reluctantly, my hand clutching the van's chrome door handle, warm from the sun, for support.

The confused ground-bass of the crowd began distantly to swell into *olés*. El Miura was working his magic.

Chichester looked as nonchalant as ever. He was dressed in a lime-green shirt over brownish trousers, with a flame red bandanna round his neck. A cotton jacket, also tan, was slung over his shoulder from his right hand. His skin had darkened, but the glossy black curls of his hair looked as well groomed as ever. The sun flashed on his gold ring as he put out an arm to lean against the wall.

'We meet again. Less unexpectedly this time. So rude of you not even to say "hello" in Granada.'

'Yes, er, hullo. Look, I expect you want your hashish...'

'Not quite so fast, Elmer.' His eyes narrowed. 'It is very civil of you to be anxious to return my property to me, but, on the face of it, a shade pusillanimous. I have seen Mr Jones in town, and Charley and Paco. And, you know Elmer, it wouldn't surprise me one bit if one or more of them wasn't quite near to us now.'

I wiped my face again. Chichester swung his coat round in front of him and for a moment I thought he was going to pull a gun or something.

The crowd fell silent.

But it was his gold cigarette case. His lighter flared.

The crowd erupted and began chanting. El Miura had made his kill.

'So I think we will prolong the charade a little longer.' He blew smoke into the air that was motionless here in the August afternoon heat—in the bull ring it again rained offerings for the rising *novillero*. 'Unlock your door, there's a good chap.'

Mesmerised I did as I was told.

'Get in and unlock the passenger's door.'

I did so, and when I looked up from leaning across to

flick the chrome lever on the other side, I saw him coming away from the trunk of the Seat which he slammed behind him. He was carrying a narrow case about three feet long.

'Right,' and he swung into the seat beside me. 'Off we go.'

I started the engine. 'Where to?'

'The Salamanca road, to be sure.'

But at this moment a wild figure appeared in the exit from the bull ring—a wordless shout and she streaked across the road, through the sunlight. Jo Tangmere. She pummelled at my window.

'Mark Elmer, what is this? Where are you going?'

I looked at her dumbfounded.

'What do you mean, what is this?' I said, winding down my window.

She stamped her foot. Bewilderment turning to rage.

'Going off with Chichester. Why are you going off with him?'

The rich voice murmured in my ear. 'A touch hysterical, don't you think? Just drive off, please. She'll get out of the way.'

And indeed I felt impatient too. 'You know very well why I'm going off with Chichester.' I took my foot off the clutch.

She jumped back and then, with a gesture of despair, shot back towards the bull ring.

It took me a second or two to get the van out—it was now wedged in by another car behind—and while I was manoeuvring a wine-skin dropped through the air and fell a yard or so away. El Miura's return of empties had become a little over-enthusiastic.

CHAPTER XV

At the bottom of the hill where all the roads leading in to Alba diverge, there was a holdup. A large lorry was crossing the bridge towards us; a bus in front of us was disputing the way. Since traffic had congealed behind both, there was a lot of hooting and blowing of whistles going on. Glancing in the mirror I saw the chocolate coloured Ford Galaxy edging out of a side-street two or three cars behind us.

'You spoke of Mr Jones and so on,' I said, after wetting my lips. 'They appear to be behind us.'

'Naturally,' said Chichester. Then as the lorry thundered by and the traffic began to move again, 'No doubt a little surprised to see us leaving together in your van, but wide awake enough to follow us all the same. Mr Jones did put you up to this, did he not?'

I couldn't speak—I just nodded.

'Of course he did,' he said.

We were across the bridge now. I turned on to the Salamanca road and looked back. At the far end of the bridge the blue van was just leaving Alba—less than a quarter of a mile behind us. I said nothing about it— Chichester seemed interested only in the Galaxy.

'Um—how fast do you want me to go?' I stammered. 'I mean, do you want me to try to lose him?'

'Good though these vans are, I don't think you could

lose that Ford. No, just proceed at a normal speed—say, forty to fifty miles an hour. That will give me twenty minutes or so, which will be ample.'

He tossed his cigarette out of the window and undid the case he was carrying on his knee. Inside was a gun. In pieces. He began to screw them together. I don't think I can begin to describe how frightened I now was. After a time the weapon seemed to be complete. He worked a ... a bolt, I suppose it was, pulled the trigger and so on, and the not unattractive smell of machine oil reached my nostrils. He pushed home, with a heavy click, a long magazine, and pushed two more into his trouser belt.

'The FN automatic rifle,' he said, with satisfaction. 'Standard NATO issue, you know. I had a devil of a job getting it, had to go to Belfast in the end and make a very hefty contribution to some prod volunteer organisation's funds. Still, I should think it will even up the odds.'

'The odds?' I asked, still trembling. 'You're not going to use it, are you?'

'Three to one old boy. Though I don't suppose Jonesy will be up to much in a showdown. Yes, of course, I'm going to use it.'

'But you told me to go to Salamanca.' I suppose I had visions of a shoot-up in the sun-baked Plaza Mayor, in and out of the porticoes.

'The road to Salamanca. In about ten minutes you will approach a hamlet called Calvarasa de Arriba. Just before the village there is a turning, a dirt road, unsignposted but in fact leading to Los Arapiles; eventually it connects with the road south to Seville. But before then, it passes through a wildish bit of country between two rocky hills. I intend to lead Jones up there and then shoot him up.'

'Ohhhh Lord!' It was all I could say.

167

'I shall tell you just before we come to the turning. I want you to take it quickly, without signalling, and then go up that dirt road like fury. We're higher off the ground than he is, and he might get held up. So much the better if he does—we want to be at least three hundred yards clear when I get out. We'll both stand a better chance if we are. Is that clear?'

I shook away the sweat and croaked assent.

'Sorry you should be caught up in gang warfare, old boy. But I think it's better like this than in a south London pub, don't you? I mean, one tries to be a class above the Kray twins and all that. How are they doing?' He craned round. 'Keeping their distance I see, but well in touch. I shall shoot that fucking runt Paco in the stomach, or lower if I can manage it.'

I must have grunted with surprise or horror.

'He carved up Caroline just before we left, do you see? Still in hospital. Took it awfully well, the old girl did.'

I remembered her. She had been really quite beautiful. The golden girl at the Putney party. A millennium ago.

'Can't let them get away with that sort of thing. I mean one expects the odd underling to get done over every now and then, but attacking one's wife is a bit much.'

Do you know, he patted my knee when he said 'underling'?

We drove on in silence for some minutes, past Saint Teresa's fountain, downhill. The ilex began to thin out. Already I could see the Arapiles, black low cliffs they seemed from here, like rotten teeth sticking out of the plain, dark against the westering sun. But there were more shocks yet.

'When Jo came out, why did you tell her she ought to know why I was driving off with you?' His tone was quite innocent. 'Not important now, I know, but I'm curious.'

It took a second or two for the meaning of the rather involved question to sink in.

'Why?' I said. 'Because she passed on my message to you, about meeting you during the third bull.'

There was a pause. Then he chuckled.

'You're a bit of a nit, you know, Elmer.'

'Eh?'

'Well. Really. I suppose you had to tumble to it that someone was keeping me informed, but why pick on her?'

My head began to swim, and I was conscious of rising nausea again.

'No, no. It was your old mate, Saul. Found me in Seville the night you spent there and offered his services for a couple of thousand. I beat him down of course. Hey, steady on old chap. Keep the bus on the road.'

He actually had to reach out and push the steering wheel.

'Don't take it so hard. Actually I remember he did say that you'd understand. Something about getting out of that school you both teach in, and since you were double-crossing me, he didn't see why he shouldn't do the same to you.'

We passed a row of cars on an enlarged layby. Children playing football. Couples walking about arm in arm. Sort of picnic spot, I suppose.

'Nearly there now. One good thing though. I'm glad Paco laid out copper Sands. Gave me a nasty shock when he turned up at that little hill village. I thought I'd shaken him off weeks before.'

And that, I thought as we approached Calvarasa, is the one possible gleam of hope—neither side of desperadoes knew that Sands was alive and well, and presumably on to them. Presumably. Where the hell was he?

'Steady now. The turning. About one hundred yards on your right. Don't slow down.'

For a moment I thought the van was going to turn over —the angle of the road to Los Arapiles was sharply acute and I took it at about thirty miles an hour. As it was the tail slewed away—I steered into the skid, felt the tyres bite again, and straightened out.

'Jolly well done,' said Chichester, with real admiration in his voice. 'Now try to keep up a real lick.' He glanced back. 'They'll be a good three or four hundred yards away now, and we'll need that.

I didn't need to be told, but kept my foot hard down. For a few seconds the van bounced and banged in and out of ruts, then, quite suddenly began to skid about again— we were ploughing through orange dust about three or four inches deep. It fountained up the sides of the car, poured like water down the windows, and pumped away from us in a great screen of what looked like noxious chemical smoke from an industrial plant.

'They won't want to get too close through that,' said Chichester, with satisfaction. 'You're doing fine. Only about four kilometres to go.'

'So long as this dust doesn't get through the air-cooling system into the engine,' I muttered. Already I had had to shut off the ventilators as clouds of it began to billow round our heads.

The Arapiles were looming up ahead quite close now— the lesser, northern one, slightly nearer and apparently higher than the greater, southern one—table-like crags with cliff-like sides, rising a good three hundred feet above the plain.

'You really can use that thing?' I asked, nodding down at the rifle.

'Surely. In fact I'm rather good with it. Actually I'm a

Terrier you know—go to camp for four weeks every year. Keeps one fit, gives a sense of discipline and all that, you know?'

Oh Christ, I thought, that's all I needed—a pedlar of hash to teenagers who likes playing soldiers and values discipline. And gun-crazy to boot.

The van thundered on between fields of dried-up stubble, without the dust getting any less. At least the road was straight. I wondered if the blue van had been near enough to see us turn and if it was following and who was in it. If Jo had not been spying for Chichester, perhaps Del was not spying for Jones. Perhaps Saul was double-crossing everybody. But then why would he come after us in the blue van? Perhaps Sime had commandeered it.

'Can you see the railway? A single line track over on our left. It runs between the Arapiles.'

'Have you been here before?'

'No, actually. Not right up. Haven't had time, but it's all pretty clear on the map. Actually I knew the ground from studying Wellington's campaigns. Another hobby of mine. Good place for Chichester's Last Stand, don't you think? Site of one of the old man's best efforts.'

The gap between the two hills was opening out ahead of us now and we were approaching the railway fast.

'Bloody hell.'

'What's the matter?'

'Look, can't you see? There's a station and a house by the level crossing.'

'Didn't you know?'

'I told you I'd not been right up. What a bloody silly place for a station, there's not a village for at least a mile and a half.'

'Does it matter?'

'Did you ever hear of a station without a telephone?'

He glanced back, but what he could see through the dust I've no idea. 'Never mind. It's too late to change plans now. We'll go ahead.'

I looked at him sharply. There was a dull fatalism in his voice which was, for a moment, almost touching. It dawned on me that he was desperate, with all the desperation of a cornered rat. Rats, however rattish, deserve some pity when cornered.

We thundered over the rails and the road angled right to run alongside a single, roofed platform. In front was a small stone house.

'Right, stop here.'

I jammed on the brakes, but before I had brought us to a standstill he was out.

'I'll take the Lesser Arapile, I think,' he said. 'Wellington did. I shouldn't stay in the van. They may shoot it up. Good luck. I'll see you later when it's all over.'

And he was off; he streaked across the line, over a stubble field, vaulted a low barbed-wire fence, and scrambled up a very steep path towards the top.

Down below, perhaps still three hundred yards away, the Galaxy slewed and rocked and lurched its way towards me through the still lingering cloud of dust we had left.

I was petrified. Where to go? I didn't like the idea of the house—it would be too good a spot for Charley and Paco to use for cover; in the end and with some desperation I scuttled over to the platform, which was a low concrete structure, and tucked myself in as closely as I could, keeping it between me and Chichester.

They must have seen Chichester scrambling up the Lesser Arapile with his gun, because they came on fast, not stopping or slowing until they had the small house between them and him. Then the big Galaxy swayed to a standstill about fifteen yards from me and the dust settled around it. I could now see Paco at the wheel, Charley with him, and the brown derby of Mr Jones behind them.

Nothing happened.

I could hear the clicking of cooling metal, a cricket, and the buzz of a fly.

There was a whirring noise and Charley's window sank down.

'Elmer. Mr Jones would like you to answer one or two enquiries for him. OK?'

'I suppose so.'

'That Chichester. What sort of gun has he got?'

'An army rifle. The sort the English army and NATO use.'

I think I heard a low whistle of surprise.

'And how many magazines?'

'Three.'

The discussion continued inside the car. Meanwhile I heard, and I expect the others did too, another vehicle approaching. I was not going to lift my head so it wasn't until it actually came alongside my van, and lying between it and the Galaxy, that I knew for sure that it was the blue van.

Del was driving. The engine died and she and Jo got out. There was no sign of Saul. Nor of Sime for that matter. They came and stood over me.

'What on earth are you doing down there?' asked Jo, arms akimbo. 'Those thistles look jolly uncomfortable.'

'You're not hurt are you?' Del asked, with more concern in her voice.

'Chichester is up on that hill with a powerful automatic rifle. He is just about to have a gun battle with Charley, Paco, and Mr Jones whom you will have noticed over there in the large American car.'

'Oh, rot,' said Jo smartly.

'Who is Mr Jones?' asked Del. 'Oh, I remember, you told me. Charley and Paco work for him.'

The Galaxy engine fired and settled down to a very low purr. Above it, Charley called again.

'Elmer. Tell Chichester when he comes down that he must think us bloody fools if he thinks we're coming against him with his gun. We'll get him in our own good time and he knows it.'

The car began to slide forward.

I'm not sure I can describe the noise Chichester's gun made: it was metallic rather than explosive, it was roar rather than a rat-a-tat-tat, it was very loud. Jo and Del went flat on their faces; the Galaxy shot into reverse and settled quite quickly on to a very flat front tyre; the rocky hills continued to echo.

Jo and Del crawled up to me. I have never seen two people keep so flat to the ground and yet manage to move.

CHAPTER XVI

Safe behind the house again Charley got out of the car, opened the rear door and helped Mr Jones out. Paco joined them. None of them seemed to be hurt. For a moment they looked at the car and we could hear the murmur of their voices but it was impossible to make out what they said. Then they went over to the house and knocked on the door. There was no answer. Paco stood back and shot the lock to pieces. They went in. A woman screamed, briefly.

I looked around, trying to make sense of the situation.

The two girls and I were tucked in against the low platform of the station—which was not really a station I would guess, but a pick-up point for farmers and so on. On the other side of the platform ran the single track line, then there was a field of stubble, and then the Lesser Arapile, near the top of which was Chichester with his gun. Looking back the way the car and vans had come I could see at the end of the platform a tall pile of sleepers, then the warning sign for the unguarded level crossing. In front of me were the two vans, covered in orange dust, mine nearer the level crossing and the blue one between it and the Galaxy which was equally dusty and had collapsed over its flat tyre like a bird with a broken wing. Finally there was the house—stone, two storeys, with a pleasant trellis supporting a vine. It was silent now, as innocent as a country cottage, while inside Jones and his henchmen made their dispositions at the windows which faced the railway line and Chichester on the hill in front of them.

'I don't think I like this very much,' said Jo.

'Couldn't we just get back in the vans and drive away,' said Del. 'I don't see why he should shoot at us.'

'He might well shoot at the orange van. It's got his hash in it.'

'Leave it and go in the blue van,' said Del.

Jo wriggled impatiently.

'I don't like the idea of losing that hash after everything,' she said. 'Anyway, Elmer, what the hell were you up to going off in it with Chichester? You weren't welshing on us, were you?'

'Christ. If you really don't know, you'll have to wait. It would take too long to explain. Where's Saul?'

'Silly rat wouldn't come. When you drove off I ran up to the bull ring and tried to get him to drive after you. He just gave us the keys and said we could go if we wanted.'

'Didn't he make any arrangement to meet again later?'

'No. That was the funny thing,' Del had taken up the tale now. 'He came down with us, collected his passport from the van and that was it. Jo was in such a hurry we didn't stop to argue. I guess he got windy.'

I didn't say anything. The dirty double-crossing twister —I'll bet he was windy. If he'd had a thousand pounds off Chichester and perhaps the same from Jones there wasn't much point in hanging about anyway. A sort of sickness began to grow in me as I looked at the girls, realised how awfully I had treated them, and what danger they were now in.

Suddenly Chichester fired again. I couldn't be sure where the bullets were going, but a ricochet whined by, over our heads it seemed. I suppose he was firing at the front of the house.

'Oh Jesus, I wish he wouldn't,' moaned Jo. 'It gives me such a fright.'

'I guess it wouldn't be so bad if he warned us first. Hey, Jo, you've got a burr or a thistle leaf in your hair.'

'Where? Oh, I see. Thanks.'

'Christ!' I exclaimed.

'What's the matter?'

'Bothering about your hair at a time like this.'

They looked at me as if I was mad.

Silence settled again. It was getting to be very hot and I felt cramped and uncomfortable. An unpleasant thought returned to me.

'Jo?'

'Yes.'

'We've had the hash, you know. We'll be lucky not to end up in jail.'

'What do you mean?'

'You remember Sime...?' As briefly as I could I passed on what I knew about Sands. 'But he is our one hope of getting out of all this now. He just has to be around somewhere.'

She didn't say anything. After a moment or two I realised that she was crying quietly.

'Honey, it's not that bad,' Del murmured.

'It is. I'll never get my kids back now.'

'Oh honey, honey.' Del put her arm round the older woman's shoulder. I remembered a grey, wet April afternoon when Jo had cried in her kitchen, and we had started to plan the whole absurd business.

A new noise in the distance, a noise that sent a sudden shiver of nostalgia through me in spite of everything else, the steady chuffa, chuffa, chuffa of a steam engine. It was a long way off and coming slowly, but soon we could see lumps of black smoke pushed into the hard blue sky beyond the house. The noise increased and here it came. A great big black monster of an engine, and blowing its whistle like a banshee for the unprotected level crossing. Slowly it rumbled by—we could see the driver and the fireman high up in their cabin, and the black smoke nuzzled down on the thistles around us. That smell brought back childhood too, and then a long, long chain—it seemed it would never end—of trundling, clanking wagons of all shapes and sizes.

Del squeezed my arm urgently.

'Look,' she hissed.

Paco had appeared in the doorway of the house and now he was snaking along by the trucks that were moving hardly any faster than him. He passed down the other side of the platform we were sheltering behind, and, as he came level with us, we could see he was carrying a pistol.

'You let on where I am and I'll kill you, see?' he hissed as he went by.

But the brake van was in view now and catching him up, and he didn't get far beyond the end of the platform before he had to duck behind the six foot pile of old sleepers just in front of the level crossing. I ducked down too as the brake van went by, but Del went on watching.

'Hey,' she exclaimed, 'did you see that?' And then in a hoarse whisper, 'Chichester. He came down the hill. As soon as the last wagon went by, he crossed the track.'

'Where is he now?'

'On the other side of the same pile of sleepers.'

'Get your head down.'

'I want to see.'

'Get your bloody head down.'

178

Another burst of shots, very short, very loud, much nearer, and then, most horrible of all, a long drawn out howl, rising higher into a terrible squeal before breaking up into retching gasps. Shoot Paco in the stomach, Chichester had said. Then a single shot that cut the dreadful screaming off with the finality of a guillotine.

We looked at each other. Both Del and Jo were ashen white, clinging to each other.

Footsteps, crunching through the dried-up grass and thistles on our side of the platform, between the platform and the road, and here came Chichester, quite upright, holding the rifle in front of him at chest height. He was using our vans as cover: they were parked precisely across his path to the house. He had lost his coat and his green shirt and trousers were dusty. He still had his red bandanna, hardly any brighter than the blood stain that was spreading down his left arm. At the blue van he lay down on his stomach and snaked himself up to the front wheel, pushing the rifle in front of him. He was only about ten yards away from us. He rolled on his side and, wincing with pain, pulled a magazine from his belt. We could hear the click as he changed them over. Then he gave us a grin.

'Sorry about this. I'm afraid you're going to be rather exposed now. Still it's not going too badly is it? I'm afraid old Jonesy extended his lines a bit then. Much the same mistake as the Frogs made.'

What did he mean? Oh yes—Wellington and all that.

We were indeed almost in the line of fire now, a fact that became hideously and immediately obvious. Chichester poked his gun out and drew three or four shots from the house which he answered with a burst of his own. One of Charley's bullets struck the rounded front fender of the van with a resonant clang and, deflected, struck the cast iron pillar supporting the platform roof above our heads

179

before whining away over the line. There was nothing to do but pull our heads and bodies in as close to the platform as we could. I scrabbled into the dust and thistles and managed to push up a feeble ridge of dirt, no more than six inches high, between my head and the house. I felt sick with fright.

It was at this moment that I became aware, with the horror that attends a visitation of the supernatural, that something was moving inside the orange van. The movement was so slight and so quick that had it not recurred almost immediately I would have thought I was seeing things: the rounded contour of someone's back, just visible about an inch above the bottom of the windscreen, someone who was in the main body of the van. The appearance was not repeated a third time though I now felt, perhaps imagined, that the van was rocking very slightly as if someone inside was moving around.

Who was it? Had Charley somehow slipped out of the house, perhaps when the train went by and we were preoccupied with Paco? Or even Mr Jones himself? But if so, why were they not even then killing Chichester whose back was completely exposed in that direction?

There was a sudden burst of more intensive firing from the house—more erratic too: bullets kicked the dust between Chichester and us, and a dried thistle head exploded. However, one got near enough to him: the tyre he was sheltering behind gave a deep sigh and expired— like the one on the Galaxy.

'Warm work,' said Chichester, and fired back. 'Look. I can see exactly the window the blighters are shooting from. I'm going to count five and then give it a really long burst. It's impossible for them to shoot while I am, and I think you'd be a lot safer behind your other van. So, all three of you, dash for it when I let go, right?'

We nodded dumbly. I couldn't bring myself to say that I thought there was someone, possibly a not friendly some-one, in my van. He counted to five and let loose with his confoundedly noisy machine gun and we ran.

We all made it safely, collapsing on top of each other, gasping with the effort, though it had only been a matter of a few yards. Certainly, this new position behind two vans felt a lot safer.

'Jesus,' cried Del. 'Isn't this just incredible? Like some spaghetti western but for real?'

'It's for real,' panted Jo. 'Think of Paco. And Chichester's bleeding quite a lot.'

'Listen,' I said, when I could speak. 'There's someone in this van.'

They looked at me.

'What do you mean, there's someone in this van?' asked Jo.

'There's someone in this van. I saw him. Two or three minutes ago.'

'Someone who wasn't there when you left Alba?'

'Yes, of course. Well. I suppose he could have been hidden between the back seats under the bedding.'

'You're imagining things.'

'I'm not. I tell you, I saw someone.'

'Well, get up and see.'

I looked at her. A flurry of shots.

'You,' I said.

She looked at me with scorn and pulled herself in more tightly behind the back wheel.

The gun battle seemed to have settled into a stalemate, each side tying the other down, neither able to make a move. At least that was my assessment of the situation at the precise moment that Mr Jones resolved it with the casualness of a man swatting a fly. He simply appeared on the platform behind us, and behind Chichester, having made a long detour from the house, across the line, over the field, and back again, while Charley kept Chichester preoccupied. His exertions in the heat had not ruffled him : he looked as dapper as ever with his wide-brimmed hat—it occurs to me that *fedora* might be the right term—his cane, and his heavy automatic pistol. He put the cane down, raised the pistol in both hands and shot Chichester six times in the back.

Then, with his cream coloured silk handkerchief he dabbed at his cadaverous brow.

The sliding side door of my van had been opened about six inches from the inside while all this was going on. I hardly noticed though Del did. She gasped, then shut up— presumably in response to a sign from inside. She was better placed to see than I. I became aware of a strong smell of petrol. The tank, I thought, of one of the vans had been holed.

Jones, with some effort, managed to get himself off the platform. With hardly a glance in our direction he walked over to Chichester's body. Charley joined him.

'Hey. Sport.'

The whisper, urgent yet so familiar, brought what surely must have been the last drops of adrenalin from my tired glands.

'Sport. Have you got a light?'

The bronzed, fair, frank face of Sime Sands C.I.D. had appeared in the open door.

'A light?'

'A light, a match. Cripes, what do pommies call them? A lucifer?'

I handed him my lighter.

Charley's voice. 'What about them then, sir? Can't just leave them, can we?'

Jones's gentlemanly accents. 'Dear Charley. Always so practical. But I'm afraid you're right. It would be untidy to leave them around and we are going to need their orange van, since it seems to be the only undamaged vehicle. It also has the hashish in it, I believe.'

Quite clearly above the faint susurration of the first breeze of evening that was nosing through the dried grass, the thistles, and the stubble, we all heard the solid clicks of ... of what—pistols being cocked, fresh magazines inserted? I don't know.

In one movement Sime flowed off the floor of the van on to the ground, unrolled himself to his full height, and with the high over-arm sweep of a first-class spin-bowler, flighted over the van's roof a large Coca-Cola bottle stoppered with a burning brand of cloth.

The flaming petrol spilled through the air on Jones and Charley and then the bottle exploded on the angle of the blue van's roof, exactly between their heads. Charley went over like a bull with the knife in his neck. Jones remained on his feet for seconds, his fine brown suit blackening before our eyes, his glasses shattered, and his hat lifting and almost floating away with the rising heat.

A lucifer to light my fag.

Then his knees folded, he subsided, and the burning hat floated down to settle across his blistering but dead face.

CHAPTER XVII

Well that was about all there was to it, apart from one or two more surprises that turned up later. For nine days I was in jail in Salamanca and it was during that time I wrote a first, much shorter version of what you have been reading. Sands found an English-speaking lawyer for us—a clever but eccentric young man called Doctor Ramón García Rodríguez who insisted that he would not be able to do his job properly without a detailed account of everything that had happened, with, as far as possible, a reasoned account of the motives behind it all.

'It sounds to me,' I had said, 'as if what you want is almost a sort of novel about it all.'

'Great. Grrreat,' Ramón had replied, thrusting his head out like a cock searching for food, and then fingering his moustache. 'You are so rrright. But it must not be a fiction, you understand. You see, Mark, I cannot plead not guilty for you—after all the hashish has been found in your van. But if I know *all* the circumstances (prodding my knee to emphasise "all") then I can pick out what I need to enter a plea of diminished responsibility perhaps, or mitigating circumstances—never mind what, we will think of something. The grrreat thing is we have lots of time, don't worry.'

Sands had helped in other ways too—extraordinarily he had managed to get bail for the girls, who were now, he told me, lodged in a cheap pension in the town. They were likely, he said, to be charged only as accessories, and might just get away with fines if they were lucky. Meanwhile the Spanish authorities, as well as preparing their cases against us, were conducting very full enquiries into the activities and deaths of Jones, Charley, Paco, and Chichester. Sands himself had had to stay in Salamanca to assist. Several times we were called as witnesses in what seemed to be a very thorough inquest.

'We', 'us' I have said, and that means Saul and I. They picked him up in the port of Málaga two days later and brought him back to Salamanca—initially on currency charges. Jones and Chichester had paid him in advance and he had a lot of money on him that he could not account for. The bastards made us share a cell, and for the first day or so it was pretty uncomfortable. But human nature being what it is we patched up our differences and by the end of the second day we were talking to each other, not that there was a lot to say. I was resolved never to trust him again.

Not long after his arrival he asked me why I was writing out such a full account of it all and I told him about Ramón.

'I think you're being a bit daft.'

'Why?'

'Well, it's an incriminating document. Supposing the prosecution finds out about it and insists on reading it?'

'Ramón said it was privileged—defence documents are.'

'I shouldn't be too sure of that. But anyhow I think you'll find it won't be needed.'

'Whatever makes you say that?'

'Never mind.'

'Anyway, it's quite fun to do.'

'Please yourself.'

He lay back on his truckle bed and continued smoking —foul local cigarettes which he bought from the jailer at five times the market value—with the brim of his hat resting on his red, peeling nose.

There must have been something psychic in the air to prompt me to ask my next question at that moment.

'Why did they pick you up in Málaga?'

The hat brim went back and he blew out a long stream of smoke that added to the general aroma of stale vegetables. Then he looked at me, small eyes faintly narrowed behind the lilac tinted lenses.

'It's a way out. A way out of Spain. Why do you ask?'

'I vaguely thought you'd head north for the Pyrenees, or to Madrid airport, or something.'

'A good reason for going back to Málaga, if that's what you or anyone else expected.'

But I felt he was hiding something.

On the fifth day Saul lost his patience.

'Why don't you ask that lawyer chap of yours to get permission to have the evidence against us properly analysed?'

For a moment I couldn't see what he meant.

'You don't mean the hash, do you?'

He nodded.

'Ramón says it will be done in a few days,' I said. 'They're never in too much of a hurry, you know.'

'If Ramón is any sort of a lawyer at all, he'll get his finger out and insist the stuff is looked at pretty bloody quick.'

I couldn't see the point of this; and Ramón couldn't either when I asked him. Nevertheless, he said he'd try to hurry the analysis along.

*　　*　　*

Two days later he was back, beside himself with glee, rubbing his hands, jerking his head out, hitching up his coat collar—all his roosterish mannerisms more exaggerated than ever. For some moments he couldn't even explain what was pleasing him so much.

'Fantastic,' he kept saying, 'fan-tas-tic. Chrrrrist, these people. Incrrrredible. Now, don't worry my friend, we have plenty of time, we will have you out of here in a day or two now. Really. No doubt, no doubt at all. Grrreat. Fantastic.'

At last he explained. He had been taken to a vault below the police station and there, in the presence of a magistrate, a senior officer of the Guardia Civil, an analytic chemist from the university, and Detective Sergeant Simes, the two green suitcases had been opened.

Both had contained a large number of brick-shaped packets, wrapped in foil and heavy polythene. Two had already been unwrapped—presumably when they were first brought in—and then loosely repacked. A new pack was taken up, carried over to the table and undone. According to Ramón it had contained a dark brownish-black, leafy substance, tightly compressed, with a rich, fresh aroma.

'I am an innocent in such things,' Ramón said, 'as far as I was concerned we were on a wild duck chase and had found *kif*.'

However, Sands, perhaps the only one there who was an expert on hashish, had been the first to realise something was wrong. With a deep frown on his face he had broken off a corner of the brick and was crumbling it in his palm. He sniffed it. The chemist too was picking it over. At last he had looked up, with a deeply puzzled expression on his face, and looked at Sands.

'Peat?' he suggested.

Sands had nodded, turned away, and his face, normally so florid, had been livid.

'Of course they are going to analyse every single package to see that it is not *kif*,' Ramón continued, 'but I don't think they'll find *kif*. Oh, no, I am sure of it. Sure of it.'

'What has happened then?' I asked.

He leant forward, gave the neck of his coat collar a jerk, and glanced conspiratorially behind him. 'You know what I think has happened? I'll tell you. Some policeman,' his eyes narrowed, 'some policeman has found the temptation too strong—they are not well-paid, they are not like the English police, incorruptible. And now I think they will let you free—to pursue the case will risk too great a stink ...'

Sime Sands had different ideas about where the hash had gone. In fact, I had quite an unpleasant interview with him. He was sure I knew where the hash was, and he felt, after all he had treated me very fairly and even saved my life, that I ought to tell him.

But of course I couldn't, and in the end he gave up. However, he had one more thing to say. We were in the same room he had interviewed me in two weeks before, when first we got to Salamanca, and still the sparrows fluttered about the little enclosed green garden behind him.

'What I'm going to say now has no material importance,' he said, and his voice took on a soft tone after all the bullying and blustering. 'That American sheila, Del Quay ...'

'Yes?'

'She's a ... a right dinkum sheila.'

'Yes.'

'Well. She asked me to say this to you. She feels a bit

bad about you, cobber, and she's a bit shy about coming to see you herself. She thinks you might take her for a drongo.'

'Drongo?'

'Creep.'

'Why should she feel that? I misbelieved her and treated her badly.'

'Yes, but she's forgotten that, and she thinks you might still reckie her as your sheila.'

'Yes, I'd certainly like to.'

'Well that's just it, sport. You see she's soft for me now and when this is all over she's coming back to England with me.'

His embarrassment had gone, and he was exuding a really unpleasant male vanity. Although no longer dressed as a hitch-hiker, he was still a great big, beefy, sunburnt, blond hunk of healthy muscle. Perhaps that's why I didn't hit him.

'Saul,' I said, when I was back in the cell. This was the day before they let us out. 'Where is the hash?'

He pulled off his hat and from inside the band pulled some scraps of white, well-folded paper.

'What are they?'

'Would you believe left-luggage tickets at Málaga railway station?'

I was quiet, for a long time. I had a lot to think about. At last he lit a cigarette, lay there looking at it for a moment, then switched his gaze to me. There was a lively, smug, little boy expression on his face.

'Don't you want to hear about it? How I did it?'

I shrugged.

'If you want to tell me...'

'I planned it ages ago. Right from the start. Well, I

wasn't going to help you make a fortune and settle for a couple of hundred quid for myself, was I? I bought my cases the day after you got yours in the same shop. Made up the peat in packets of foil—I'd seen hash from Morocco not long before and I just had to take a chance that yours would be done in the same way. One afternoon I nicked your V.W. key and got another cut. There was always a chance Del would see the cases on the way down, but I reckoned I would co-opt her if she did. In those days she seemed fonder of me than you. But actually she never saw them. I kept them under cushions and rugs. She was driving the orange van, and it was in the orange one that we slept. On our way out through Málaga I dropped them off at the station while she was sending postcards. Coming back was trickier. First of all I had to create a situation where I might get the chance of getting at your van with you and Del elsewhere.'

He puffed again, and coughed.

'So that's why you overplayed at the Málaga Customs,' I said. 'You wanted to be busted so we would have to go on into the town without you.'

'That's it. It was still tricky though. They let us out at about half past one on the second day. I managed to persuade Del to sit in a café with cool drinks while I said I was checking out the van to make sure the Customs had put it together right. Even so it took me nearly an hour. Still, she swallowed it.'

'And Jo and I were having lunch almost in sight of the car-park.' I remembered that foul paella. 'We could have come out at any time and caught you at it. What would you have done then?'

Saul stubbed out his butt and grinned through the dissolving smoke. 'Done? I would have had to do something? That was the beauty of it all: you couldn't touch me, I had nothing to lose, and I could have threatened to blow you at any time.'

'So you left the hash in Málaga, came on with us, and started taking money from Jones and Chichester as well as me, telling them where we were going.'

He sniggered. 'Actually Jones was paying me before we left England. Chichester found me on the camp site in Seville and chipped in then.'

I got off my bed and walked round the tiny cell, giving his chair a kick as I went by. He watched me warily— as well he might.

'How did you expect it all to end?' I sat on the bed again, chin in my hands.

'Well I rather hoped there would be an outright winner out of Jones and Chichester. To him I would have sold these tickets. No point in being stuck with the hash in Spain, and no way of getting it out, and no sure market at the other end. But then in Alba, during lunch, I was up near the bull ring and saw Sands with about six guardias all messing about your van, trying to get in. I realised he must be the law, and they were on to us, so I thought I'd stay away, stand a bit further off. Pity you missed the fourth bull: it wasn't bad.'

I remembered death in the late afternoon beneath Los Arapiles, and I shuddered.

'What are you going to do now?' I asked, after a moment.

He swung his legs off the bed, pushed back his hat again and looked squarely at me.

'I'm glad you asked that,' he said. 'We've still got to get that hash out of Spain, and I can't think of a better method than the Mark Elmer-Jo Tangmere tried and tested smuggling device. And I'll play fair with you, Mark. One quarter of the proceeds, less any expenses I run into trying to sell it. That's a hell of a lot fairer deal than you were giving me.'

I felt very, very tired. It was not a hard decision to make.

'No, Saul. Cut Jo in again if you like. She needs the money to get her children back and so on. But I don't need it. Not really. I'll sell you the vans though.'

'You're going back to Ventleigh?'

'No, no. No. I think I'll stay here for a bit. There's an English Centre where they need teachers. Ramón says it's easy to pick up private lessons. Yes. I think I'll stay here in Salamanca. It's a nice place.'

I thought for a bit about what he had said, about Málaga, having another go at getting the hash out, and so on.

'A quarter?' I repeated.

'Ah, so you are interested after all?' He looked up very quickly.

'Oh, dear me, no. I just wondered who the fourth share was for.'

'Why, Del, of course.'

'Saul?'

'Yes?'

'You didn't know then that Del is knocking about with Sime Sands now?'

A long silence.

'Is she? Is she?' He smacked the wall with his palm and slowly that awful snigger welled up from the back of his nose somewhere, spread itself through his sinuses, exploded through compressed lips—a paroxysm of delight. I didn't know what to think.

'That girl,' he managed to splutter at last, 'that girl is marvellous. Bloody marvellous. Bloody, fucking marvellous.'